MW00653960

Contents

1. Saved by Beings from Inner Earth

An escape *into* eternity, or *from* eternity? With this thought I awoke from my meditation.

I might have been asleep or awake. Sometimes it's difficult to tell the difference between dreaming and reality. You can actually experience reality in your sleep. Intangible things become tangible there. For me, it was a strange journey. And for me, it has become reality. But you are welcome to doubt my story — until it can be proved. I have no proof ... yet!

A tall, young man with fair hair, cheerful blue eyes, regular features, and a shapely mouth — a handsome, young man, in fact — had appeared while I was meditating. He started talking, and in my head I could hear every word he said. I was amazed!

"Hi Mariana!" he said. "My name's Timothy, but I'm called Tim. My surname is Brooke. Originally I'm from Seattle, USA, but I've 'emigrated,' and these days I live inside the Earth. You probably won't believe me at first, but I think I can convince you. That's my mission. It's time for people on the Earth's surface to know that we exist.

"Now I'm going to tell you my story."

* * *

My father was a sea captain. He owned a small cargo boat which plied its trade along the coast between Seattle and Vancouver, Canada. I was brought up as a sailor, pretty much against my will, even though my mother didn't want me to go to sea. She thought her constant worry about my father was enough.

My mother was Swedish and my father of British stock. That's why I'm bilingual. They met on a cruise in the mid-20th century. Then I came along, and later on, my sister. All three of them are dead now, but I survived a shipwreck when I was nineteen. In spite of Mother's tears and pleadings that I wouldn't go to sea, I was father's first mate by this stage, instead of staying in high school. Father was a resolute but fair man, and I loved him.

A terrible storm swept relentlessly over us, with waves as high as houses. Our little boat had weathered storms before, but this was like a volcano. We were close to the coast, which was rocky and inaccessible. Father wanted to anchor as close to the shore as possible, so we steered towards land. Our cargo was timber and it was heavy, but we didn't get very far before we were caught in a whirlpool which lifted the boat like a glove and threw it against the nearest cliff. I remember a terrible crash and my father's otherwise stern face being close to mine.

"I love you, my boy," he cried, with tears in his eyes. "If we ride out this storm, I'm never going to force you to go to sea ever again."

Those were his last words. The ship was torn apart, and I was in the sea, clinging to a log floating on the cold waves. I remember passing out. Father was gone, and the four others in the crew had disappeared.

Suddenly, I felt someone human nearby, and a boat was carrying me steadily forwards. Was this death? I lay in the bottom of the boat and tried to raise myself up on my elbows, but fell straight back down again. A friendly face with clear-cut features and long, fair hair bent over me, and at first I couldn't tell if it was male or female. I soon realized it was a man.

The boat entered a kind of well-lit tunnel decorated with paintings. It wasn't long before we were moored at a jetty. The fair-haired man and another one with dark hair lifted me up and helped me ashore.

"Where am I, where's my father? Where are the rest of the crew? Did the timber go down?" The questions gushed from me in a rush.

"Your father couldn't be saved, nor the crew or the cargo. You were clinging to a log which brought you straight to us. That saved your life. We were on the lookout for wrecked ships because of the storm. You're inside the Earth now. Welcome!" The man spoke excellent English.

"I'm Mannul Zerpa, and I'm taking you to our world for some rest."

When I was younger, an old sailor told me many stories. One of these was about a world that existed inside the planet, and it completely fascinated me. Of course, I'd thought it was just a sailor's yarn. And yet here I was, in the middle of it, right in the middle of an old sailor's tale! I pinched myself hard to make sure I wasn't dreaming. This couldn't be true — but it was.

"When can I return to Seattle?" I asked.

"You'll have to take that up later with someone else. Look around you! You're walking on solid earth."

The light was strange when we came out of the tunnel or hole in the rock where the boat was tied up — a strange glow in a strange summery landscape. I had left Seattle on a dark November morning, windy and drizzling. There had been leaves on the ground, and the sky was gray.

Here the air was clear, with a friendly sun beaming down on us. Glorious flowers lined our path. There were green trees and bushes everywhere. It was like a beautiful morning in a Canadian forest. I had been in forests like this many times with my father and uncle when I was younger, but this seemed sparser and lighter somehow, with more flowers.

"We're just coming to the village where you're going to stay," announced my fair-haired savior, with a smile. My savior, literally!

"I have to thank you," I stammered. "You saved my life. It's just that I feel so confused. I'm actually inside the Earth, below the soil, in some kind of village in a farming area?"

"You'll find out more when we get there," Mannul informed me. "I've saved lots of people from drowning. Your ship isn't the only one to go down outside these mountains. But it's only the sea out there which is treacherous, the sea which belongs to the outer Earth. In here it's calm and always summer."

And I had to make do with that.

We walked through the most beautiful landscape I have ever seen, before reaching a village with tall, round buildings. They seemed weirdly luminous, probably because of the stones they were made out of. I could hear birdsong in the luxuriant trees, and I saw squirrels and a small hare which crept behind a clump of grass. It was like the outside Earth,

7

yet very different. Somehow, it was too perfect, like a film!

The houses surrounded what seemed to be a small market square, with a well in the center. We entered one of the houses. A hall with an arched roof led into a semi-circular room with floor-to-ceiling windows. The furniture in the room was what I would deem modern — comfortable, beautifully-designed chairs and tables, yet different from furniture on Earth. Everything glowed, as if the furniture itself and the surrounding walls were alive. And the roof! It didn't exist! It was open at the top, with sunlight filtering softly through woven leaves and branches.

Mannul gestured for me to sit on a sofa by one of the unglazed windows, where I could see the amazing view outside. The friendly, fair-haired man disappeared after placing a cup in front of me. He would return soon, he said. He told me to drink up before his return.

I tasted the drink. It was wonderful, like a pale wine with a slight tang of honey. The first mouthful shot through my body like an arrow of fire, and I came around at once. Good grief, I thought, I'll be drunk! But I wasn't, even after drinking it all up. However, I did experience intense clarity of thought and great wellbeing.

When Mannul returned, he wasn't alone. With him was a man who was at least six and a half feet (two meters) tall. He had gleaming, long, brown hair and was clean-shaven and lithe. His huge, beautiful eyes were set in a youthful face, yet I got the feeling that he was older than time! I stood politely and bowed, and he gave me a friendly smile and hugged me.

"Welcome to Wonderland underground, Timothy," he said. "I know how you got here, and now I'll tell you where you are."

"Are you a Wise Master?" I interrupted, "I've heard people like that exist inside the Earth." The man laughed heartily.

"There is wisdom everywhere, young man," he responded. "The man who believes himself wise is stupid. Stupidity always tries to mislead wisdom. But if you're seeking wisdom, you need only look around carefully. Nature is full of wisdom which surface-dwellers are doing their best to destroy."

"Then, who are you?" I asked, inquisitive as usual.

"My name is Dariel. You don't need to know more than that just yet. I'm one of the nine on the Committee here. We bid you welcome, and wonder if you would like to stay a few days as an honored guest from the surface."

I bowed again and accepted the invitation. You don't turn down an invitation like that.

"Will you help me to get home afterwards?" I asked. "My mother is bound to worry that I've drowned like the rest of them."

"Yes, we'll help you get home, if you still want to go." Dariel gave me a long, keen look. "We don't force anybody to stay here, but few return home, and those who do are never believed when they tell people about us.

"This is a pleasant place to live. We don't fight about money, and most of our needs are taken care of. We keep track of the surface and the people there. We know that their supposed development has only brought disaster. Everything is easier here. You're going to love it."

Dariel stooped and took my hands. He looked right into my eyes, and I was filled with an indescribable inner peace. I was still grieving profoundly for my father and missing my mother and Littl'un, my sister. But, in a flash, the grief and longing lessened, and I wanted to learn more about this peculiar country I was in. It was as if I had been stroked softly by an angel's wing, leaving me happy and at peace. In the distance soft music was playing, not at all like modern music from above ground, more like Mozart or one of the old Masters.

"Mannul will take you on a tour of our borders, beginning a few days from now. First you will visit Telos, which is where surface-dwellers end up if they happen to fall into our world.

"Timothy, I'm your friend. Please call on me if you need questions answered or help of any kind. We'll meet again when the time comes."

2. Agartha —
A Paradise Inside the Earth

"A country where sorrow doesn't exist!" I exclaimed, as Mannul guided me through a village that was laid out like a huge smile. Mannul grinned too.

"You're right," he replied. "But most people who live here are just ordinary people like you and me. There is sorrow, but it is treated differently here. You allow it to dominate you, but we take control over sorrow and setbacks. Friendly hands reach out when you need help — physical or psychological.

"On the surface, you haven't discovered the joy of helping each other. Your thoughts are on money. Help costs money, and not everyone can afford it. But Tim, everyone has a heart, and that costs nothing. You only have to listen to it. Your heart gives you good advice, but you have to talk the same language. Experience and understanding will help you."

I don't know what happened next; it all went so fast! Mannul held my hand and I felt like an apprehensive, expectant seven-year-old, going off to school for the first time. I didn't have much time to see the scenery which whisked by. There seemed to be water below me at one stage, and small, white geese (as they were known at home) bobbing on the dark-blue water. Then there was sand on golden sandy beaches, and finally emerald-green grass. At last, with a slight thud, we came in to land.

"Look around you!" Mannul burst out.

I did. If Mannul hadn't been holding on to my hand, I probably would've fainted, but there really was cause for my confusion. The air and lovely surroundings were alive — not with a peaceful, eternal breathing, but completely tangible, lively, and almost wild. Every single bush, tree, and flower produced noise, bordering on a cacophony. Small figures sailed smoothly to and fro and round and round. They wound their way between the plants and onto the plants and inside them.

The summer meadow was alive in more ways than one.

Elementals and people crowded together here. I could see people — adults and children — and I could hear rousing music. Everyone was dancing.

"Are they having a dance right in the middle of the morning?" I asked, slightly shocked at such enthusiasm so early in the day.

"Of course!" replied my guide, looking at me as if I was weird. "When someone wants to dance at work, we organize a hop and sing."

"Does anything get done, then?" I ventured to ask.

"More than if we didn't dance," was the retort. I sighed. This was another country, and I needed to be open to new ideas. All countries have their own customs, and this was as true on the inside of the planet as on the outside. There were huge differences.

We stood awhile, watching the dancing. It was like folk-dancing really, although I've only seen Canadian and Swedish folk-dancing, so I don't claim to be an expert. The musicians danced as they played, and their fiddles and other instruments that I didn't recognize sounded like folk-music from Dalarna, Sweden, where my grandmother lives. I hadn't visited my grandmother for a few years, but I remembered how wonderful Swedish midsummer was. This was similar, but without any drunkenness or fighting.

I looked inquiringly at Mannul, and, chuckling, he took my hand and swung us out among the dancers. Soon I was holding a soft, female hand and watching a smiling young girl swing me around. But the dance didn't last forever, regardless of my desires. My "underground" guide pulled me away.

"We have to get on!" he exclaimed, laughing at my disappointed expression. A completely lovely landscape passed before my delighted eyes, and we arrived at a village. There were fewer houses, but built in the same style: beehive-style, as I called it, although rounder than beehives and without tops. I wondered if they had rain, storms, or snow here.

"No," Mannul read my mind (that too!). "We have a perfect climate here. We have what you would call early summer all year round, and pretty much full bloom."

"How come you have a perfect climate when we have rain, snow, and storms on Earth?" I wondered in surprise.

"Doesn't our weather seep through somewhere?" Mannul guffawed. I couldn't understand what he was laughing at. There was a bench nearby, and he gestured for me to sit down. This is how he explained the amazing climate underground:

"Everything has to do with belief," he said. "We feel completely safe here. There is no fear, worry, evil, envy, or jealousy. We have learned to live in complete safety and believe in an eternal Force which is always here to help and protect us. Negativity disrupts the lower atmosphere and the stratosphere. Weather patterns reflect patterns of thought.

"Destruction on the Earth's surface means that meteorological forces are equally destructive. They are affected by the ambiance on Earth, which is far from harmonious. There is religious conflict. Envy and suspicion, fueled by money and drugs, destroy rather than build up. If we weigh the good and bad on Earth, my dear Tim, good loses every time."

"Good grief!" I exclaimed incredulously. "You don't mean that the weather depends on how people think? Surely the weather is regulated by other forces entirely." (I couldn't think of anything other than the National Weather Service, but felt that wasn't quite what I meant in this context.)

"Here you could say that we're in the lap of the Earth," said Mannul, smiling. "This in itself represents security, because your adverse conditions can't penetrate the thick crust between us. We honor, thank, and caress Mother Earth literally every day, and in return she provides protection and love. You surface-dwellers would feel better if you focused on your counterparts in Agartha (the name of this interior world) and took strength from here when you are depressed or troubled. If only you would ask us for strength."

"We don't know about you," I replied bitterly. "How can we ask someone for help if we don't know they exist?"

"Then it's time for us to approach people on Earth," was the reply. "But we don't want to encourage those who sow the seeds of dissent and discord. That is why we have shut ourselves off for so long. And, by the way, what about that God you worship? He's worshiped with great pomp the whole world over. You pray to him, fight wars on his behalf, argue about him, and lay all the blame at his feet. What kind of a religion is that? You might think it's logical, but we don't. This is why it would be difficult to allow Earth people here, unless they are specially chosen, or are people who arrived as you did."

"I want to return to the surface and tell everyone about you," I said.

Mannul just nodded, and helped me up from the bench.

I couldn't see many people in this village. There were children playing in much the same way that children on the surface play. There were sandpits and swings, and adults to look after them.

There were pools where children were swimming. The pools were wonderful, with slides which children love. Leafy vegetation surrounded small, sandy slopes where the children could slide into the water. There were exciting, winding, stone steps to scamper up and down, and more besides. The children seemed to live in a fairytale land.

"There are quite a few children here …" I began. I wondered how they got here, but I didn't dare ask. Mannul burst out laughing, which I was getting used to.

"Listen to me, young man!" he snorted wildly before continuing. "Do you need sex lessons? It's exactly the same here as on the surface. But we call it Love here, which is rare up there. Sex is depraved there. Here it's something positive that we respect. We don't have marriage here, but a 'union' of body and soul. And a union is always a good excuse for a party."

"Infidelity, mistakes, indiscretions, divorces …?" I continued.

Laughter bubbled from Mannul as he answered, "You've got it wrong again, son. Those words don't exist in our vocabulary. Up there you live like you are just bodies. We are souls with a much higher level of consciousness. But we have as much fun as you do — the difference is that we stay together all our lives."

"For hundreds of years," I chuckled. "You'd really have time to get tired of each other. You need to try different things ... even with sex, right?"

"I don't see why." Mannul really didn't seem to understand. "That's not how Love works here, anyway. Come on, let's carry on. We're going to a kind of symposium that they're having beneath Mount Shasta in Telos. They're discussing surface-dwellers, so I want you to come with me."

I was filled with curiosity. Maybe I could reach the Earth's surface from there. Yet, Mount Shasta was in California, and I wanted to get home to Seattle. There would be flights, but I had no money. I said as much.

"Don't worry, son. We'll sort it out. If you want to go home and the others agree, we'll find money for the journey. Let's do one thing at a time."

I thought about the incredibly cute girl I had danced with, and considered staying. Mannul read my thoughts easily, but just squinted at me and grinned.

"Her name is Sisilla," he said.

3. An Important Mission for Tim

The rest of the journey was by hovercraft, as it is called, and was double-quick. I didn't have much time to see my surroundings, just glimpses of mountains, forests, and lakes which flew past — or which we flew past. It was more fun than flying in a plane. We landed with a splash in the canal. Not with a hefty thud, but gently, like a dancer in Swan Lake.

Here, finally, was a house which looked like a house. It was low and elongated, built in the round, but I couldn't see a roof here either. It was a shimmering pink — unusual for a house. Around it were masses of beautifully arranged flowers, in all colors imaginable.

"This is what you would call the Town Hall. We call it the Meeting House. Sometimes we have planning-meetings and organize help. This is where you can ask for help getting home."

We went inside. I was overwhelmed by the beauty I encountered inside the building. The walls were painted with lovely natural images, and between the flagstones on the floor grew low, green plants with white and yellow flowers. There were tall, gracious, fair human forms moving around everywhere.

We ascended a spiral staircase in the center of the room. The building didn't have a roof, and the top floor consisted of a sort of suspended platform. It didn't move, which would have made me seasick. Mannul smiled, took my arm, and led me to a large, airy, apparently floating room. There were nine people there, men and women. They were sitting in a ring of comfortable chairs, each with a small green table before them. There were flowers everywhere. The walls were of woven branches, some with exquisite blossoms.

When they saw us, someone brought two chairs and asked us to sit. That was just as well, as by now my legs were like jelly. I noticed a venerable person sitting in the center, his blue eyes focused on me. His hair and beard were long and white, yet his face was unwrinkled, and he looked youthful and happy. He raised his hand in greeting, and I did likewise.

"Welcome, young man from the Earth's surface," he said in a clear voice, in English. "I'm Arniel, leader of the symposium. We hope you are happy and will stay with us."

"I'm amazed and delighted at everything that I've seen," I replied. "However, I miss my mother and my sister, and I would like to go home and visit them first. Afterwards, I would like to return here for good."

"Your wish will be granted," said Arniel. "There is one condition. We want the surface people to know that we are here. You are welcome to return, but first you must spread the message of our existence."

"They'll never believe me," I mumbled, but Arniel held up his hand.

"Don't give up, whatever they think. If you get into difficulties, we will come to your rescue. It is time to tell the surface people that we are here and they are not alone. We have no wish to partake in their pollution and other misery. Please emphasize that. If they carry on, they will cause their own annihilation, total extinction. This won't affect the planet itself, just the people. It will be serious, and it will happen soon."

"Can't we be saved?" I wondered, terrified.

"We hope so. We're working on helping the Earth, as otherwise we may be affected too. You must be our messenger, Timothy."

"I'll do my best," I stammered.

The imposing Elder held out a small whistle to me. "If you're in trouble, blow this. You won't hear anything, but the signal will reach us at the speed of thought. Don't lose it."

I bowed and thanked them over and again until Arniel, laughing, stopped me with his hand. "Don't worry about money, my son. Mannul will give you plenty. You may need to stay a good while. He will take you as far as the portal on Mount Shasta."

Mannul pulled my sleeve, and I bowed slightly more quickly this time. I didn't have time to see who the others were at the green tables, but I'm sure I didn't know them. I felt completely dazed.

18

"You'll need some suitable clothes," said Mannul, looking at my thin, white shirt and tight, blue trousers. He hustled me out of the building, down a narrow alley, straight to a tailor's. It couldn't have been anything else; there were clothes hanging everywhere. A man emerged from the interior and greeted Mannul warmly.

"Bring the boy some nice clothes," said my guide. "Give him a bag filled with all he'll need for an Earth visit. And one of those wallets that they use above ground. I'll put money in it for him."

"Am I going to California right away?" I asked.

"Yes. There are regular flights to Seattle from there."

"What if I want to get back?"

"We'll cross that bridge when we come to it. Let's do one thing at a time. The tailor will outfit you first. I'll wait for you here."

I returned to my guide wearing jeans, a pale blue pullover, and a navy jacket, and felt slightly awkward seeing Mannul's ankle-length gown. At the same time, I felt great, and incredibly pleased to be going home to my nearest and dearest. Mannul handed me a bulging wallet. It included my passport. I have no idea how he had gotten hold of it.

"It's a new passport that we made in surface-style. Don't you think we know what you need in order to avoid the long arm of the law?"

Well, obviously, only I hadn't gotten that far. I stomped after Mannul, my backpack a secure weight on my back. We wound our way through the picturesque town of Telos and reached a tunnel. There were some small vehicles there, and Mannul and I got into one of them. He pressed a couple of buttons, and it started immediately.

"Don't give up, however unkind that people are," he warned. "And if, against all odds, you meet an Earth girl, tell her about us. She's only worth bringing here if she believes you."

"I might want to stay at home," I replied. "My mother may need help. She'll be living on a widow's pension, which won't go far."

"I'll ask the stars for guidance," said Mannul, giving me a shrewd look. "You have to come back, to turn in a report to Arniel, if nothing else. If you want to return to the surface afterwards, we'll discuss it then. I don't think that's what the stars have in store for you."

"What stars?" I asked, looking around the tunnel. There was only a weak, flickering light from one or two lanterns. But Mannul just laughed, and the tunnel grew much lighter.

The truck stopped in front of a long staircase. I gave my kind companion a hug and started up the stairs, my steps quickening as I climbed. Finally, I stood on a platform, and an iron door opened onto what I knew at that time as Life. I walked slowly out into the rain and wind on the great mountainside. Mount Shasta witnessed yet another small human leave its dark embrace and grope his way to what is known as reality.

4. Sad Tidings in Seattle

I don't remember coming down Mount Shasta, but at the foot of the mountain was a small town, complete with motels and shops. I traveled from there by bus and taxi to the nearest passenger airport and was soon settled in a comfortable seat on a flight to Seattle.

I was thinking about my mother and sister, and there was a furtive tear on my cheek when the stewardess arrived with the beverage cart. I remembered my mother as a fairly tall, beautiful woman having curly, blond hair with a few gray strands framing a smooth, rosy face with eyes like violets. My dear mother wasn't just attractive, but sensible, warm, and loving!

And red-headed, mischievous Littl'un, a younger sister to be proud of, but who still needed the protection of an elder brother. She was always much too willing to get into mad scrapes with her friends. When I left home, she was seventeen, and worryingly popular with the boys. My family was everything to me, and I missed them intensely.

The closer I got to home, the more worried I became. I was arriving, of course, with a well-filled wallet, which I would have to explain. I was smartly dressed and much wiser than when I had set out. But you don't earn money on the high seas. Well, I would just have to come up with some yarn before I dared tell the truth. Then I remembered that actually, it was the truth I was here to tell, and, sighing, I finished up the generous amount of food served on the plane. To my relief, it wasn't beef, but finely-sliced chicken with plenty of vegetables. After a vegetarian diet, your stomach reacts to what we call normal food, especially meat.

I knew Seattle airport well. Seattle is on the coast, and our house is near the large harbor where the cargo boats are moored. Our house, like many in the area, had its own jetty. As I alighted from the airport taxi, I was whistling the happiest tune I knew. What a great feeling! I was back at my beloved childhood home.

I rang the bell. I kissed the door handle and rang again. I rang the special code which my sister and I used. Nobody answered. Mother and Littl'un were both out, and I didn't have a key. Then I heard a woman's voice that I recognized. It was the kind lady next door, known as Big Tillie. I turned around and there she was.

"Is that really Timothy Brooke? Weren't you drowned? Are you a ghost?"

"I'm alive and kicking. I didn't drown, but all the others did. I haven't had a chance to get in touch with my family. Do you know where they are?"

I thought Tillie was going to faint, and I put my long arm around her shoulders to support her. She burst into tears.

"You've been away three years," she sniffed. "Your mother and sister are both dead. Your sister secretly got married just before the terrible news came. She died giving birth six months after her marriage. Your mother sickened after hearing about the shipwreck and died a few months later. I think she died of sorrow, after losing her entire family. The house has been up for sale for a long time, but it has not sold, so I guess it's yours. Your brother-in-law, Bertie, moved to Vancouver. I think he remarried.

"I've got the address of your mother's lawyer. You must find out if your mother left a will. Come in and I'll make some tea to fortify you. You can stay here until you get yourself sorted out."

I went with kind, old Tillie. A cold hand gripped my heart. I had no family left. There was only me. I was the loneliest person in the world. I sank down on Tillie's sofa and cried. This time they weren't tears of happiness. I felt sorry for myself, though I knew it wouldn't help, and I was overwhelmed with grief. I still had a difficult mission to carry out in spite of all this bad news.

Tillie was a great help. She called the lawyer right away, and I took a taxi to pick up the house keys. He had not been able to sell the house without proving there was no-one to inherit. The lawyer had been in no hurry to investigate. He seemed relieved that I had turned up and that Tillie could vouch for me. So I had a roof over my head.

It felt weird entering the empty house. My old bedroom was dusty and untidy, just as I'd left it. Littl'un's room had changed. There were baby things in it, including a cradle — probably our old cradle. On a table an unfinished baby cardigan was thrown, likely the work of my mother.

I sat down in the cozy living room with its big open fireplace and wondered what I should do. Should I sell the house or keep it as a kind of sanctuary? I decided to keep it for now, until my journey began. I lit a fire, sat in Dad's armchair, and slept.

Tillie and her husband were great. Harry, who I remember from childhood as fairly taciturn and morose, was almost over-friendly, thumping me on my back and welcoming me. Harry and Tillie owned a fish market nearby and it was doing a roaring trade, as it always had. They were well off.

Tillie decided that I couldn't cook for myself, and she turned up regularly with delicious meals for me. If it was beef or pork, I was forced to throw it away. After the years (which felt to me like only days) in Telos with simple vegetarian food, I could no longer eat meat.

One day, after a short while, which I was counting as a sort of holiday, visiting my family's graves and walking in nearby fields and woods, I was sitting and talking to myself in the kitchen. "If only I knew where to start!" I sighed.

Tillie, who was doing my washing in the basin in the next room, cut in immediately. "What about your old friends?" she called. "I know! I'll ring the local paper and tell them you've returned from the dead. Hmm, 'risen from the dead' sounds even better!"

"Yes, but the people who turn up will probably be the ones I least want to see," I protested. "There are a few who would rather I had drowned, and I know exactly who they are."

I'd told Tillie and Harry about Telos. Their reaction to the story was very simple. Harry laughed heartily, thumped me on the back, and exclaimed, "You spin as good a yarn as your father, my son!" Tillie made no comment on my story, but told me instead how much my mother had missed me and wept about the shipwreck. It didn't exactly make me feel good to hear this.

But Tillie was right. She rang the paper, and it wasn't long before a reporter appeared. I'd planned to tell the truth to the reporter, a middle-aged lady with short, mousy hair. She listened intently, made copious notes, and asked about my childhood. That made me suspicious, but I carried on telling her about Telos.

Imagine my surprise and consternation when the article appeared a few days later alongside a large photo of me with the sea in the background. The story of my childhood was pretty much as I had told her, but my visit to the Earth's interior was blamed upon a concussion I had sustained as the ship went down and I hit my head on a log. This was mainly because she didn't want to alienate her readers. It was a horrible article, but it served its purpose.

There were phone calls the same day as my proud appearance in the paper. I was overjoyed at one of them. My best friend from school, Matthew, wanted to meet up as soon as possible. He was still in Seattle. He was a dentist, and invited me to dinner with his family. He was married and had a small daughter. I rushed over to their house at the earliest opportunity.

Matt and I hugged each other. He was as tall as me, but stockier, and his red hair was thinning. His hair was the reason we used to call him "Red Matt." He still had freckles and his eyes were just as gray and lively as ever. His stomach was rounder, suggesting satisfaction.

His wife, although obviously pregnant, was as pretty as a doll, with brown eyes and frizzy brown hair. Their little girl had inherited her father's red hair and freckles. She was attractive already, and she would be beautiful later. My thoughts went to my unruly, red-headed sister, and I sighed deeply.

Matt and his family lived in a fairly large house with a lovely garden. The abundant Seattle rain streamed peacefully from the sky, forming pools on the leaves. I finally felt at home.

"Well, where have you been for the last three years?" asked Matt as we sat on the porch with a drink. "The newspaper article was a load of bunkum, wasn't it? The Earth can't be hollow, although our geography teacher used to joke that it was."

"Can we talk about this after dinner?" I asked in reply. "I'm not sure you're going to believe me."

Just then I had the same strange, inexplicable sensation I had experienced a few times since coming home. It was like an intense heat searing through me, and lights flickering before my eyes. I knew it was Mannul sending this energy. As we had said our farewells at the portal on Mount Shasta, I had been overwhelmed by this feeling.

"Your head is lit up!" little Elinor's voice exclaimed. Matt's daughter was standing by my side, looking with interest at my head. She was four years old. Matt had married before our boat sank.

"Come and eat! It's ready!" It was Nancy, Matt's wife, calling.

I took Elinor's hand and followed Matt into the dining room. "I think it must've been a lamp on the porch shining behind my head, Little Red Riding Hood," I whispered to the child, who pressed her lips together and shook her head.

"There's a tall man behind you," the peerless child continued. "He says he's your friend, but he won't tell me his name. You're Swedish, aren't you?"

"Yes, I'm half Swedish, and half from here." I grinned, glad to be changing the subject. Matt's daughter was obviously clairvoyant. I planned to mention it to him after dinner. He shouldn't let her be afraid of it; it was a gift. It was a rare and wonderful gift, which could easily become a burden.

Nancy was a good cook, and we ate a delicious fish dish, and afterwards lemon pudding which melted in your mouth like clouds. When we were sitting in the living room and Nancy had taken her small daughter upstairs to put her to bed, Matt asked, "Have you let your grandmother know that you're alive?"

I turned hot and cold. My beloved grandmother! How could I have forgotten her? I'd been home nearly a week! Grandmother lived in Sweden, in Dalarna, in a village called Floda. She was an amazing old lady, in her 70s, always interested in the supernatural, who told fortunes with cards, and the like.

"Do it first thing tomorrow!" Matt urged, seeing my confusion. "I realize that you've seen some strange things, but you seem well enough, not ill or emaciated. Unusual experiences can be confusing and make you forgetful. Tell me about it!"

"I'll go and see her," I said earnestly. "My grandmother, I mean. She'll believe me. I'm going to tell you my story and leave you to make up your own mind what you believe. But I am absolutely in my right mind and in good shape."

I told Matt my story. Matt topped up our coffee and brandy, but didn't say a word. His gray eyes widened and reminded me of when we were boys off on some forbidden prank. I didn't leave out any details about Telos. I'd nearly finished when Nancy came and sat down with us. Then I was silent, looking imploringly at my old friend.

"Well, what do you think?" I asked. Matt scratched his red mop and smiled.

"I believe you, Tim," he said after a pause, while Nancy looked questioningly at each of us in turn. "I believe you, with reservations. Tomorrow is Sunday. I'll come by about 10 o'clock and we can go for a walk and talk this over."

5. The Trip to Sweden

"Is it really you, Timothy?" My grandmother's voice was full of laughter and tears. "My only grandson, are you alive? Why didn't you ring before? Is it really you, or just someone's idea of an unkind joke? If it's really you, Tim, you should come and visit as soon as possible."

"I'm on my way, Grandmother. We were together four years ago, so you'll recognize me when you see me. I'm looking forward to seeing you. Toodle pip, Grandmother!" Toodle pip was something we had always said when I was small. I said it so she would know it was me for sure. Her happy laugh at the other end confirmed that she understood.

When Matthew came, he told me that Nancy had been very inquisitive after I'd left. She wanted to know the whole story. She heard a condensed version, and accepted it readily.

"I think she has second sight," Matt confessed as we walked into the forest.

"Like Elinor," I added, smiling.

"I'm inclined to believe in Telos and everything that happened there," said Matt, his eyes glinting playfully, "until there's proof to the contrary. As far as my wife and daughter are concerned, I've known for a long time that they're both intriguingly different. I believe in the supernatural, and yet I don't believe. Worlds beyond this one must exist. It would be arrogant of us to imagine otherwise."

I reached my hand out toward a branch of the lime tree we were passing. To my surprise — not to mention Matt's — the branch came away from the tree and flew into my hand.

Matt stopped in his tracks. "Are you a wizard as well?" He frowned. "What happened? What did you do?"

"I'm as flabbergasted as you are," I exclaimed. At the same time, I wondered if Mannul's embrace on Mount Shasta hadn't been more than just a hug. This might be a message from him or the man Elinor had seen behind me. I smiled and thumped Matt on the back.

"Do you believe me now?" I asked. "I'm flying to Sweden first thing tomorrow."

"I'll take time off and drive you to the airport," replied Matt, "unless you're going to teleport! Yes, I reckon you've seen some strange things. Take good care of yourself, and come home soon. When you get back, I think you should buy a car. You have to get on the road and tell people your story."

Next morning, sitting on the plane to Sweden, I thought about the reaction of my childhood friend. His last words at the airport had been, "I'll be there for you, no matter what! Let me know everything's okay!" I knew that he was one of the few who would believe me. A hollow Earth was too much for people to get their heads around, and if I was unlucky, there could be an uproar. Yet I was convinced that Emilie, my grandmother, would believe me.

When the taxi drew up at my grandmother's house in Floda, which I hadn't visited since I was ten, Grandmother rushed out with open arms. After a keen glance and a cheerful chuckle, my only living relative on the Earth's surface hugged me. Tears ran down her worn cheeks, and she whispered repeatedly, "You're alive, you're alive! If only your mother had known. She died of unnecessary grief."

"But Grandmother, you know as well as I do that our journey through life is preordained," I remonstrated as we entered the house arm in arm. I stole a glance at her. Her white hair was elegantly trimmed. Her face was carefully made up. You had to look for wrinkles. She was plumper than I remembered, but not fat like Tillie at home. I felt no surprise entering her beautiful living room and sinking into an antique armchair.

"Tell me everything, Tim, even if you've spent three years in a foreign brothel. You know I'm not easy to shock." She laughed delightedly at her audacity and served me coffee from a Thermos jar. I assured her that was not the case, but that I had spent three years in another country inside our own Earth. At first, she seemed flabbergasted, but then she jumped out of her chair and hugged me.

"Oh, Tim, how wonderful!" she gasped. "I've always believed the Earth was hollow, ever since I was at school, but everyone assured me it was impossible, as the planet was full of molten lava and fire, just like a volcano. I've never believed the scientists were right on that score. Tell me every single detail you can remember, my dear!"

I talked and talked. In the end, I was so homesick for Telos that I had tears in my eyes. I reached out and took Grandmother's hands.

How can I fulfill my mission?" I groaned. "Nobody is going to believe me, apart from you. And you're not like … other people!"

"We'll have to make sure they believe you," Grandmother promised me. "I know plenty who will. Tomorrow we'll make a start. But now we're going to have a lovely dinner, and in the morning you can sleep in. You've had a long, tiring journey. I'm going to tell you about your mother and sister.

"Your brother-in-law would never believe you. He's an unpleasant man and I can't understand why your sister chose him."

Now it was Grandmother's turn to talk, and I was glad I came as fast as I could. It was nice to know about Mum and Littl'un. I needed some kind of closure on the part of my life which was over now. New horizons were opening up and it was time to make plans to carry out my mission.

"You know, Tim," Grandmother remarked after dinner, as we were lounging in front of the fire which I had helped light. "I have never told you everything about myself. I'm a medium and I help people, and actually I have quite a good reputation, which I'm grateful for. I lecture about other worlds, other planets, and cosmic consciousness. I help people find their inner selves, listen to their own hearts, and straighten out their minds."

"Do you see it in the cards?" I interrupted her.

"No, I see it in their eyes," she answered calmly, smiling. "Their eyes tell me what their lips cannot convey. I can see their auras, which is always helpful. Otherwise, I have nocturnal friends — guides, as they're called — who help me. They appear in the daytime too, but I have to be in a trance. I have a spirit guide, you see, who has been with me through various lives. I listen to him and talk to him sometimes."

"Jesus?" I asked.

Grandmother smiled wanly. "No," she replied. "Too many claim to be in contact with Jesus. It's very contemporary to be in contact with Jesus and God. My guide is called Melchizedek."

"Melchizedek!" I interrupted again. "You have a great guide in him, an Ascended Master arisen from the dead."

"I know," my grandmother resumed calmly, a smile twitching at the corners of her mouth. "He's wonderful, and incredibly wise. He was an alchemist, and Abraham's teacher. Now he's my teacher." She chuckled in that special way. "Well, my grandson, do you believe me?"

"Yes," I sighed, impressed. "Of course I do. Can you also see him?"

"I see him with my inner eye. He's taught me a lot, I have to say. He was a comfort when my family died, and I'm convinced he helped to save you. He didn't dare tell me, though. I would have done all I could to bring you home. In my heart of hearts, I cherished a hope that you were still alive somewhere, washed up on a far-flung shore."

I have never understood the trend for Ascended Masters that many people indulge in, but when my own grandmother professed to having one, I was forced to acknowledge that these high Masters may have contact with humanity. I'm not really interested in this kind of thing, and I would rather cultivate the sort of knowledge I came across in Telos. But we'll get to that later, when I tell you about returning there. I had learned to live in the present during my stay in Telos, as the concept of time there is as free as the sweet-smelling air, but now I had to conform to Earth time.

Grandmother gave me a diary. It is a necessary piece of equipment on Earth.

6. An Impossible Mission

Grandmother had a number of spiritual contacts and she was definitely a good connection for this odyssey, as I considered my task. She rang all her acquaintances who had occult interests and invited them to a meeting at her house on Saturday.

Many were interested when they heard it was about Hollow Earth. I would tell them about the Inner Earth city of Telos. Twenty-four people agreed to come, and on Saturday they crowded into the spacious living room. Grandmother served coffee and cakes, and everyone jostled around me, asking about Telos.

I gave a short lecture and answered questions. One man caught my attention. At first he kept in the background, but later he asked if I was planning to stay in Dalarna or if I would be willing to talk about Telos in Stockholm. I jumped at the chance.

I realized quite soon that Telos only interested those familiar with parapsychology. The first lecture I gave in Falun attracted an audience of seven. My new acquaintance, Carl-Olov Strand, generally known as Chaos, became a firm friend who dedicated himself to guiding me through the ordeal that is parapsychology. He was divorced, recently retired, and lived in a house just outside Floda. This meant we had ample opportunity to meet.

It was difficult to convince some people that there really is a whole world inside the Earth. Why had nobody else discovered it before? How could they be sure I was telling the truth and wasn't a "spiritual conman?"

Chaos comforted me when I had doubts about my mission. He had a doctorate and was very intelligent. His presence at my lectures should have brought me credibility. Believing in an inhabited world,

Agartha, inside the Earth was too extreme. To some, it seemed like a swindle, and if I didn't cease my ridiculous nonsense, I should be put away, either in a mental institution or a police cell. I was under constant threat, and when the newspapers got wind of it, things got worse. Chaos was my self-appointed body-guard. He was quite well known, an academic, responsible for many interesting articles, but he was taking a scandalously serious interest in pure science fiction.

Grandmother was a constant source of encouragement, and her loving defense of her only grandchild was commendable. She didn't care that I was unpopular with some of her friends and most of the inhabitants of Floda.

It was so bad that I bought a dog, a Great Dane, two years old, trained to protect. I called him Titch, as he was so huge. We became the best friends in the world, eating and sleeping together. His constant companionship engendered respect and admiration. I bought him from an old lady who could no longer walk him. My grandmother organized it, of course. Soon it was a common sight to see me walking Titch, who reached above my waist. He was gleaming black and inspired respect. Titch still lives in Telos, but I dare not bring him to the Earth today, as the time may not be right for him.

With their tiny, short skirts, their heavily made-up eyes, and weird hair, none of the girls on Earth impressed me. Many of them were beautiful, and, actually, there were some "normal" ones, but I sensed that they only pretended interest in my subject to go to bed with me. I don't think the Earth has bothered to take care of its inhabitants properly — or vice versa, which is preferable. In other words: I didn't fall in love with a girl on the surface, despite being surrounded by them.

Grandmother, Chaos, and Titch were the only ones I talked to and who helped me express myself. One evening, as we were sitting in front of the fire as usual, Grandmother inquired, "Timothy, are you planning to stay here and carry on like this? Is this what you envisioned? You've been here three months, and you know you can stay here as long as you want, but Swedes basically still don't believe in the existence of Telos. I have approached some contacts in television, and they aren't remotely interested. You don't have any proof to back up your claims. You can prove you were shipwrecked and saved by persons unknown. Your denigrators claim it may have been an unknown tribe in the Canadian mountains. I hear all sorts of things when you are traveling, and it worries me. Swedes always need proof, you know."

"Proof," I muttered. "Aren't I proof enough? I can make things move by mere thought, and influence people mentally, if necessary ..."

"People don't want conjuring tricks," said Grandmother impatiently. "The only proof you have of your identity is your passport. We need much more than that, Tim. We need the knowledge and insight to understand. It would be easier to prove that there is life in outer space than inside the planet! I can contact beings in outer space through my guide, Melchizedek, if I want. But I want to sort you out first. You have a mission, and I have promised to help — and that's what I'm going to do."

I walked further and further with Titch. I could let him off the lead in the woods and he would stay close. This gave me time to reflect. I thought about the Beauty I'd met dancing in Telos with Mannul. It cheered me up, thinking of her, of Mannul, and the amazing "Wonderland." At the same time, I felt oppressed by my Mission. I decided to call Mannul. I needed help. I blew the little whistle, and Mannul came.

"What's the problem, Tim?" he asked. He appeared to me in the forest, wrapped in a green cloak, merging with the moss and trees.

"Weeeell!" I drew it out. "I don't know if I should stay here or return to Agartha."

At this juncture, Titch returned from a run. He stopped in his tracks when he caught sight of Mannul. I thought he would start barking, but Mannul bent down and patted him on his gleaming doggy neck. Titch pushed his great head against Mannul, and lay down on the moss at his side.

"You are welcome to bring him to Telos when you come," Mannul commented, and that made me want to leave immediately. But Mannul raised his hand.

"Really," he remarked, "you had no need to call me. This is your problem alone. It's up to you to choose. I can't give you any advice other than to listen to your heart. You will know. I can't tell you what is right or wrong; you have to choose. Use your common sense and don't get caught up in your emotions."

This was a sore point. I always have problems making decisions, as I'm scared of flapping off in the wrong direction. I'm quite impulsive and have to restrain myself sometimes ... well, always!

"Thanks," I said slowly. "Sorry for calling you unnecessarily, but you've helped me decide." I looked up, but Mannul had gone. Maybe he had been a hologram, limited by time and range.

Titch didn't react to Mannul's disappearance. He yelped, and dug his nose so hard into my armpit that I almost toppled over. It was his special sign of love, and I laughed and started running homeward.

I hadn't bought a car yet, as Grandmother had lent me her Audi. Besides, I was going to wait until I got back to Seattle. Home, sweet home — how many homes have I got? I drove the Audi as fast as I could (way over the speed limit) to Djurås to see Chaos, with Titch panting on the back seat.

7. Tim's New Family

I decided to return to Seattle. I may have planted some ideas which would flourish in Swedish minds. I decided to write an article about Telos, and Chaos promised to print it in one of the big daily papers.

It was tough leaving Grandmother, my only living relative. I promised to ask if she could come to Telos. That's what she wanted now. She was tired of spirituality in Sweden, such as it was, as it was so superficial. I was worrying about Titch being caged on the plane and going into quarantine in the US, but then I realized that Mannul could help. I would be returning to Telos soon, anyway. He came, to my relief, and took Titch, who was no problem. Both of them disappeared in a haze.

When I reached Seattle and jumped into a taxi, I felt like a stranger. I began wondering if I shouldn't have gone straight back to Telos. But first, I wanted to see my closest friends, Matthew, Nancy, and Elinor. Nancy may even have had her baby by now. I decided to stay a month in my childhood home, and then it would be time to return inside the Earth! I missed the wisdom which pervaded Telos. Neither Swedish nor Canadian learning was enough for me. Not that Seattle was in Canada, but it wasn't far off. I'd always thought of myself as a Canadian, ever since I was a child.

Before I went back to my house, I called on Matt and Nancy. I was dying to tell them about Sweden and Titch. We pulled up outside their house, and I asked the taxi not to wait. It wasn't far to walk home from there, and I didn't have much to carry. The lights were on and I rang the doorbell. It was only eight o'clock, but it took Nancy a long time to open the door. Her eyes looked red, as if she had been crying, and I couldn't see Elinor. Nancy was slim, so the baby must've come.

Then I heard the terrible news. Matthew was dead. He had been killed in a car accident. He was hit by a drunk driver on his way home from work. His car had spun around, gone into the ditch, and smashed against some rocks. He was rushed to the hospital, but didn't survive.

Nancy cried in my arms, and I tried to comfort her with all the love I could muster. We were sitting, talking about Matt, when Elinor padded downstairs, barefoot and in pajamas. She threw herself on me, crying, "Daddy's dead. I haven't got a daddy any more. I want a daddy! Can you be my daddy?"

Nancy tried to calm her down, and in the end, I carried the four-year-old up to bed. At her bedside was a cradle with a doll in it. The real baby had been born prematurely and didn't survive. It happened just after Matt's death, so they were grieving for two family members. When Nancy went downstairs, Elinor whispered in my ear, "I saw that Daddy would die soon, and then I saw that you and I and Mummy would move some place with loads of flowers."

I was startled to hear this. Could I take Matt's family to Telos? That's what happened, and something else too! We took another relative with us to Telos.

I rang Grandmother to say I was fine and that I was planning to depart soon for the world inside the Earth. Grandmother was on the verge of collapse. She'd received threats after the last meeting of her parapsychology friends. She'd mentioned me and Telos, believing her friends to be interested. Some unauthorized person had wormed their way in and was horrified at the discussion. She had received lots of hate mail, and even a death threat. She should have gone to the police, but that would take time. Could she come with Matt's widow and me?

I asked Mannul for advice in the usual way. Of course my grandmother was welcome in Telos, was his joyful reply.

I rang Grandmother and told her to pack as fast as she could and get the earliest possible flight to Seattle. It wasn't long before she was at my door with a whole truckload of luggage.

The journey to Mount Shasta was tough, but we were rewarded by the sight of Mannul, who met us at the hidden entrance to the subterranean Wonderland. He brought Titch with him, and I was literally bowled over by his exuberant greeting.

Elinor and Titch fell in love at once. Titch became a gleaming black comfort in all our lives. Nancy had been overjoyed when I invited her to accompany me to "Wonderland." But there was a lot to organize before we left.

After this visit to Sweden and Seattle, I've kept away from the outer world. What I'm going to tell you now is solely about Agartha.

8. Back Underground

"Look at all these flowers!" was Nancy's first exclamation as we stepped out of the small trucks which had brought us from Mount Shasta. Elinor and Titch immediately romped around on a lawn full of daisy-like flowers of pink, yellow, and white. Mannul chuckled at them.

"It's great to see happy children," he said. "I bid you all a warm welcome to our land. We'll do our best to make you happy here."

My grandmother, Emilie, looked around and then exclaimed, "This is nothing new! I recognize this from my dreams. It feels like I'm on the right side of Dream-world now."

Our luggage (there was quite a lot of it) had come in a separate truck from the tunnel and was being loaded into one of the vehicles which floated above the ground. Mannul called one of these over and asked us to climb aboard. It was nothing new to me. Nancy and Elinor watched in surprise as I stepped into the spacious vehicle. Mannul and I were able to transport ourselves differently, but I didn't want to leave my friends and grandmother alone in a foreign country.

The vehicle set off towards their new home. I call it a vehicle, as the transport in Telos is neither car, nor boat, nor airplane. We call them hovercraft, as hover is what they do.

We hovered a moment and "Aah, oh, look, gosh" were the only words my friends could utter. We stopped in front of a house, one of the roofless, round houses which make up the town of Telos.

My grandmother clapped her hands in delight. She had greeted Mannul like an old friend, and thanked him for his brilliant rescue of her beloved grandchild. I was a bit embarrassed, but at the same time proud of my beautiful, intelligent, and loving grandmother. When I had told her about Telos back home in Sweden, she did not seem at all surprised. She had already dreamed about a place inside the Earth. She seemed quite at home here now. Mannul gazed at my grandmother in a strange way, as if they already knew each other. I didn't ask. There would come a time when all these questions would be answered. It was always like that.

Elinor, who, by the way, was known as Ellie, was first to rush through the open door. There were no dividing walls in the round house, just as there was no roof. It was just one big circular space. There were portable screens in case a separate bedroom was needed. In the center was the great "living room" which you furnished in accordance with your desire. There wasn't really a kitchen, just a place near the wall where cups and plates were stacked on a shelf above an ample table with drawers. I already knew this, but naturally, it seemed strange to the two ladies.

"There's no oven or sink or dishwasher …" came from Nancy. I could see she was desperately trying not to laugh, yet at the same time seemed on the verge of tears.

Grandmother was calm. "Nice not to cook," she said, sinking into a comfortable armchair in the central section. There were flowers in abundance, even indoors. The various areas of the room were divided with flowers. It made the house cozy and welcoming.

"I need to pee, Mummy!" Ellie had rushed around inspecting everything, but hadn't found the bathroom. I laughed, and took her through a side door. The bathing facilities were there. There was a kind of toilet where bodily waste disappeared and dissolved ingeniously. You washed and bathed in a pool belonging to the house.

As for food? You ordered it via a machine in the kitchen area, or went to the house it was served in, which I'll tell you about later. You pressed a button and then decided whether you wanted foodstuffs or a prepared meal. This involved the power of thought.

"There are people who work in this town, then," observed Nancy as we walked around the garden and Titch marked his favorite spots. "Where do you live?"

Suddenly, full memory of my previous time in Telos came flooding back in. "I have my own house not far from here," I replied. "Everyone works, Nancy, but in a different way than you are used to."

"What do you do?" asked Nancy again.

"I'm a type of healer. I help people. There is actually a sort of hospital here, but not like those above ground. We show people how to help themselves."

"What if Ellie fell and broke her leg?" Nancy was stubborn.

"Then I'd cure her pretty quickly." I smiled. "Anything can be cured in our way."

"How come there's such a difference between the surface and inside the Earth?" Nancy wondered. "We've got the same soil around us."

"But," I responded, "there's a difference in age between your soil and our soil. The souls which inhabit this part of our globe are ancient. Some of yours are ancient too, but here the ancient wisdom is established."

There was a yell from the garden, an unmistakable Ellie-scream. We rushed out and, to my delight, saw Ellie face to face with a kangaroo, complete with a joey in its pouch. Nancy laughed.

"There are plenty of wild animals roaming freely here, and they are not at all dangerous," I said, as the terrified Ellie hid behind her mother. The kangaroo stayed, and I went and patted it. It was used to people and, looking at Ellie in surprise, it hopped off into the trees.

"People and animals are friends here," I explained to the frightened four-year-old. "You have to learn not to be scared, and to wait for the animal to come and let you pat it. Never pat wild animals on the head, but on the neck or back, and don't rush at them. Always stay calm. Animals can sense that."

Titch sat by the door as if he was guarding it. He was naturally a great guard dog, but as that wasn't necessary here, I decided to keep him just as a pet. He liked Grandmother, so he might spend some time with her.

I went inside. Grandmother was still in the armchair looking a bit lost. "Oh, there you are, Tim," she said, smiling. "Shall I find myself a corner here?"

"No," I replied. "You're going to have your own house next door to me. Let's go now, as Nancy has plenty of unpacking to do."

We walked on the grass between spaciously arranged houses and soon reached my abode and the house next door where Grandmother would live. She was in rapture. It was a pale pink house with silver gables — roofless, of course — with roses and climbing plants everywhere.

"Goodness gracious!" repeated Grandmother a number of times, as we looked around. "I'm going to love it here."

I really hoped this was true. Although Telos has a friendly atmosphere, it is full of adventures too. There is wilderness outside the town, and wild animals live close by, but not with humanity as such. There are various tribes who have moved here and live their own lives. They have their own traditions, which we may find difficult to understand. The rest of us in Telos don't get involved — why should we? There is a law here giving humans the right of freedom. Freedom is more important than anything. I told Grandmother this.

"Freedom of the soul is a good thing," she agreed. "But it's difficult to experience complete freedom while in a community with fellow humans. There are different types of freedom, Tim. You have some kind of laws here, don't you? What are they?"

"You'll see later, Grandmother." I smiled. "We don't need to discuss that now. But one thing you do need to know: We have the most extraordinary library imaginable, unparalleled on Earth. The books are kind of plays performed for you. It's difficult to explain; you have to see it. I promise you, you won't be bored here. Taking a 'taxi' to the library costs nothing, and is quick."

"Great!" Grandmother said. "May we start a complete tour tomorrow, so I can get acquainted with as much as possible of this part of our planet? Today I want to rest in my new home, inspect the garden, and feel that you, and Titch, of course, are close by."

"That's quite a comprehensive tour you're planning," I laughed. "But first you have to see my house and find your way there, because the houses aren't laid out like on the surface. Up there they are crammed together, but here they are well-spaced. There's room for a garden and a vegetable patch. If you can't manage to grow food yourself, someone will help. Let's go to my house and have lunch. I've shown Nancy how to order prepared food. We'll have dinner together, too."

Grandmother and I sat discussing the differences and comparing everything to life on the surface.

9. A Tour of Telos and Its Vicinity

"What's the time, Mummy?" The question accompanied a huge yawn. A tousled, red-headed girl stretched and sat up in bed. "Isn't it light!"

"Our clocks aren't working, darling!" Nancy sat on the edge of her daughter's bed. "I haven't a clue what time it is, as yesterday evening it didn't get dark when we went to bed. But I feel rested, so I think you should get up now. There's a lot to see and find out, like whether you can start school here. You ought to soon, and I wonder if there's a good kindergarten, and where it is. If there's no time, no day and night, how are we to know when to get up and go to bed? I need to talk to Tim."

"What a weird breakfast, Mummy! I want normal milk and cereal. Have you made coffee for yourself?"

"No, there's no stove. There was a plate of the local food here when I woke up. Tim probably arranged for it. It looks nice, a bit like green meatballs. We've got bread as well."

"Is there any cheese? I want some cheese!"

"Eat what there is, Ellie. I'll talk to Tim about food, I promise. Come, let's go for a dip in the pool."

Nancy sighed. It was very different from America. How could her daughter ever understand the huge, revolutionary differences between here and their home in Seattle? Right now the most important thing for Ellie was cereal and milk and the chocolate drink she was used to at home. Nancy missed coffee and the generous breakfast she was used to. Yesterday evening, my grandmother had shared the food she'd brought from Sweden, and it was wonderful.

"Lots of things are different here compared to what you're used to!" a cheerful voice said. It was me, Tim, arriving with a basket of locally produced food. "Imagine you were shipwrecked on a South Sea island

45

and you had to eat the same as the local inhabitants. You'd have to get used to it. It's the same here. You'll get used to the food, and you won't want anything else. That's what happened to me. I soon forgot all about ham, lamb chops, and rare steak."

"Shut up!" Nancy was cross. "I'll soon get used to it and probably Ellie will too, but I keep asking myself if I've done the right thing in coming here. Ellie is having this pushed on her."

Now it was my turn to get angry. "That's a bit strong, Nancy. This is Paradise. Chocolate muffins, English marmalade, and jellied veal are not part of it. The most important thing is not what you eat, but what's inside you. Your inner life, I mean: Love, joy, beauty, friendship, and compassion are important here. You'll meet people who can explain this better than I can. Grandmother is outside talking to Ellie and Titch. We're off on a tour now."

Nancy was sulking, but she followed Titch and the others into the hovercraft I had arranged for. As soon as they were seated, the vehicle rose a few feet and hovered above the ground. The houses were widely spaced in a beautiful area and there were no roads, just a few paths trodden through the grass. Not many, and they didn't go far.

"On the Earth's surface, we eat food which is processed and transported long distances," I said, regarding Nancy and Ellie gravely. "Strangers made that food, and it is imbued with their personal energy. Food on the surface contains a hodgepodge of energies, not all of them clean and pure. Here we eat food grown nearby, in our own neighborhood. It hasn't been processed, and is completely natural. We enjoy cooking and creating with it, without by-products. Heating up food destroys its nutritional value, but hard beans and such need cooking and home-grown spices."

"Where do you get hold of it?" asked Grandmother. "Are there central food stores where you can obtain it?"

"Oh yes!" I exclaimed. "You can either walk there or take a hovercraft. They're not far away. Not everyone has their crops ready at the same time."

"But I haven't seen a single person working here," Nancy commented. "Do invisible slaves do all the work for you?"

"Everyone works four hours a day," I replied. "We work intensively, without a break, to get everything done. Everything is well-organized, but there are absolutely no slaves. We take time off without needing permission. Because everyone has a job they enjoy, this is never a problem."

"There must be factories," Nancy complained. "That's often monotonous and dirty work."

I began to find my best friend's pretty, little wife slightly trying, but Ellie came to the rescue. "I can make paper from sand and water," she claimed, eagerly.

"We use hemp." I smiled. "It makes great paper! You can see how it's made."

"It's lovely to feel this sun on my face," Grandmother said suddenly. "It doesn't feel as if I'm going to get sunburn."

"You won't here," I explained, putting my hand on hers. "Our sun is electro-magnetic based, and doesn't produce dangerous rays."

"Is Telos big?" asked Ellie, stretching out her arms as far as she could and standing up in the vehicle, which rocked. If I hadn't caught her, she would have fallen out.

"Sit still, Ellie," I warned her. "I'll tell you how big Telos is. Telos isn't a country, just the main town in this part of the kingdom of Agartha, which exists under the entire surface of the Earth. That's really big. There are countries and states and different kinds of people, just like on 'normal' Earth."

"It sounds wonderful!" Grandmother's eyes glittered and glistened in the calm, pleasantly warm sunshine filtering through the trees, brushing our faces with its silken rays as we bumped along on uneven air thermals. The vehicle stopped in the air a moment, and then sank down to land a few inches from the ground. I stepped out and my three comrades followed.

Water glittered close to where we'd stopped. From the green grass on the shore, a small bridge led to an island which seemed connected to both sky and lake. Shimmering blue above and fading into emerald-green, it appeared as a rare jewel floating on the waves. In a way, it was just that. I padded barefoot across the bridge, less than twenty feet (six meters) long. The green grass sparkled on the other side, too. I had been here many times before, and knew my way in this amazing place.

The small pavilion was surrounded by a sea of flowers. Above it was an arch, carved with the word "Porthologos." This was one of the innumerable entrances to the enormous library which spread out under Telos. The pavilion was incredibly beautiful, with walls of precious stones, and inside a staircase leading downwards. It had a church-like interior, the stones reflecting and refracting the light in a multitude of nuances. My grandmother, Emilie, stopped, and clapped her hands in a typical gesture.

Nancy looked around like a tourist. "Where do the stairs go?" she asked. "Down to Hades, huh?" I didn't appreciate the laugh that accompanied her question.

Ellie didn't know what Hades was, and was hopping around without a care in the world, now and then touching a beautiful gemstone. She certainly didn't look like someone who had been forced to come here, I thought, as I went downstairs and Titch sneaked past me. He didn't like going down stairs slowly. I held Grandmother's hand, although she was as nimble on her feet as a twenty-year-old. I saw Nancy holding on tightly to Ellie, though the child didn't appear at all scared. Maybe it's Nancy who is scared, I thought. I was right. Her fear would surface again and again.

It was light and warm downstairs. Mannul was standing in the beautifully-sculptured doorway to welcome each of us with an embrace. Ellie got the biggest hug, and was lifted into the air by the tall man and danced in a circle. She put her arms around his neck as he set her down.

"I like you," she said. "You and Titch are my best friends!" Titch was already off into the immense archive with his tail wagging happily, way in front of us.

"We're in the biggest library in the world," called Mannul, in English, which was mostly the language we used, unless I whispered something to Grandmother in Swedish. English was her favorite language, and she talked and read it fluently.

"We can find out about almost everything here, whether it's the past or present of our own Earth, or elsewhere in the Universe," he continued. "Instead of books, there are actors who answer our questions. They act out scenes as answers. Just wait!"

"There aren't any books here?" cried Nancy angrily. "It's not a library, in that case!"

"Ask something!" I suggested. "There are books here too, but plays are more common."

"Was there really someone called Merlin, or is he a myth?" Nancy immediately asked.

"Come with me," cried Mannul, and he led us up some steps to a wide corridor with doors on either side.

I have to describe what it's like in our special library, which was originally an enormous cave. There are small stages everywhere, combining film and reality in an endless store of knowledge. There's a network of passageways and rooms which you need a guide to show you. We have plenty of guides, some elementals, and some holograms.

All our inhabitants are eager to learn. By living in a symbiotic relationship, we benefit from collective knowledge, but this can be transferred to individuals. And questions are welcome — that's what the library is for.

I tried to explain all this to Nancy as we followed Mannul down the passageways. As we stopped near a booth that was reminiscent of a theater with comfortable seats, Merlin greeted us from the stage. He told us that he had really existed, and had been an important, respected — but envied — wizard. He performed some magic tricks, which made Ellie scream with delight. Suddenly, there was a small, white rabbit on her lap, and equally suddenly, it was gone again.

He described his life to Nancy, who was amazed, then he acted some scenes and showed film clips. The widely-renowned magician concluded, "I am neither invention nor impostor. Nowadays, the world on the surface is ruled by swindlers who, consciously or unconsciously, make it their duty to mislead people.

"But a new era is coming. The surface is about to undergo a cleaning and a cleansing like never before. There will be pain and innocent sacrifices, but the result will be reconstruction in the name of Love and truth, converting the planet into a carrier of light. I, Merlin, proclaim this in the name of the eternal Truth." The stage darkened.

We were mesmerized. Then Nancy got up and burst out, "But it's just a play. It's not like that in reality. It was the actor's role to express it that way. Can we see some books now?"

I was astonished, and Grandmother was too, as she pinched my arm and seemed shocked. Ellie started crying.

"It was all true, Mummy. Tell me it was!"

Mannul lifted the little girl up and whispered in her ear. A big smile replaced the tears. I'll never know what he told her, but it cheered Ellie up, which was the important thing.

It took a long time to see a just small part of the library. Sometimes there were wider galleries hung with lovely paintings, where tables, chairs, and couches invited rest.

We stopped when we were hungry, and refreshing drinks appeared. We didn't see anybody serving, but Mannul explained that he had arranged for the refreshments on arrival in one of the galleries. Ellie didn't protest; she just consumed what was on offer with delight. Nancy carefully tried a mouthful before swallowing it, as if scared she was being poisoned.

"We can test it on Titch, if you like," I suggested spitefully. "He can stomach anything." Grandmother gave me a warning look, but Nancy took some bread and fed it to the dog. He gulped it down and looked for more. I gave him some, of course.

Ellie was beginning to tire, and I asked Mannul if we could stop. He led us straight to an exit, where a lift took us back outside. Out there, it was as light as day.

The most difficult thing about living here, I think, is the lack of day and night. The friendly sunshine is eternal and unchanging. For surface-dwellers it's difficult to acclimatize, but in the end you get used to it.

10. A Fond Reunion and a New Acquaintance

Whether it was day or night, Nancy yawned all the way home, and Ellie slept on Mannul's lap. Grandmother, Mannul, and I decided to go for a walk when we got back home. I have no idea where Mannul lives. He's always there when you need him. Nancy said a sleepy good-night and carried in her slumbering daughter.

You have to find your own walkways, as there aren't any roads. I learned fairly soon after coming here how to walk around, or hover around, in Telos. You can go by hovercraft, but you can also hover yourself, only a few inches above the ground, but even so! It's a great feeling. Grandmother couldn't do it yet, so we walked arm in arm over the grass, while Mannul hovered a little way in front of us. Suddenly he stopped. We could hear music and boisterous singing. A host of dancing couples appeared, lovely and lithe.

"Gorgeous!" was, of course, my grandmother's comment. "How wonderfully in step they dance."

"Feel free to join in, if you want to," suggested Mannul. "We'll meet up by that tree over there when you're tired."

He disappeared into the whirling dance and Grandmother and I followed closely on his heels. It wasn't easy to define the dance in words. It seemed as if everyone moved separately to the music, yet there was harmony, as if there was some general plan to it all.

"Hello again!" Behind me was a voice I recognized and had longed for. My exquisite friend, Sisilla, took my arm and danced off with me.

"Long time no see," was the extent of my repartee.

"Time doesn't exist here," she said, smiling. "Here it's always just

NOW. As long as all of us think positively and devote ourselves to enjoyment and Love, our NOW will continue. On the surface, you lack joie de vivre, and you have turned Love into something profane and unethical. We like working. We like relaxing. We like helping each other. We like walking in our beautiful forests. We like meeting people we love."

She dropped my hand and disappeared in the crush of dancers. I called out to her and tried to struggle through the veils and flickering hair, in vain. Instead, I bumped into Mannul, who took me over to a large tree. Grandmother was sitting there talking to a man who seemed older than the others around us.

"This man is a relative newcomer. He's only been here two months, by your time," Mannul recounted. "We hold meetings for people who haven't been here long. I can tell Emilie more about that."

"Yes, maybe I should attend?" I wondered.

"No," replied Mannul, to my surprise. "You came here by a different route and were looked after by Arniel and me. We've other plans for you."

"I hope Sisilla is included in them," I muttered. "Will I meet her again?" Mannul grinned, but didn't answer. We caught up with Grandmother and her new friend at the tree.

"This is Lex," she said, and the man beside her bowed slightly. "Though actually, his name is Alexander." He was quite tall, with thick, white hair and appeared to be in his 60s. He had friendly, sensible brown eyes and a smile which displayed even, white teeth. His skin was quite brown, like an Indian or Native American. He had quite a prominent nose which suggested Native American.

"I haven't traveled as far as you have to get here," remarked Lex in faultless English. "When I heard about Agartha at home in Peru, I knew I had to come. But it's not the easiest place to get to. It feels like being in quarantine, as I've just told this delightful new-arrival. I'd like to show her a little more of this beautiful country, as I've traveled fairly extensively."

"We've met before," said Mannul taking the man's proffered hand. "I thought my newcomers would like to meet you, Lex."

"I heard there was a newly arrived young widow and child," said Lex. "Where are they?"

I greeted him in the ancient Indian way, which he returned. Then we shook hands. "You'll meet them tomorrow," I answered. "Be prepared for lots of questions."

"I'm used to questions," he observed. "I was a kind of modern Indian chief in a small Peruvian village with ancient traditions."

"You'll have to tell us more about that," I said cheerfully, taking Grandmother's arm. "If you can find your way to my house, let's meet after a well-deserved sleep."

He nodded, and I said goodbye to Mannul. We would meet again the next day, after I'd been out with my friends.

With his help, we planned a scenic tour in an area unknown to me. I had expected Nancy to be delighted with the planned trip. Instead, her face was sulky, with traces of tears. She sank down onto the sofa and asked me to sit next to her. Ellie was playing in the garden.

"I have to get her into school," Nancy complained. "I can't cope with her at home all day. I don't have time for anything else."

"You don't need time to do too much," I said comfortingly. "There's no school here, as such. Children can be educated at the library if their parents desire it. They learn to read and write, and other useful things, but it's not education in the same way as on the surface. If they aren't keen to learn, then the teachers talk to the parents about trying alternative methods, like painting, crafts, singing, and stories. But first you need to talk to a teacher at the library, and introduce your daughter."

Nancy started crying and threw her arms around me. She actually climbed onto my lap, and I was forced to get up to free myself from her indiscreet advances.

"I thought you liked me," she sniffed. "I thought we would get together in all this unknown ..."

Luckily, she was interrupted by Ellie, who came rushing in with another girl of a similar age. "Mummy, I've got a friend who speaks English too. She's called Wendy, like the girl in Peter Pan, and she talks to fairies. We're having fun!" Everything was said in one long rush, and then she gave me a hug.

"Ellie, I don't think we're going to stay here." Nancy's voice was frosty. "There's no proper school, and I miss so many things. I don't like this country. I want to go home to Seattle. Our house is just as we left it. I never put it up for sale, just in case! We haven't been away long."

"But Mummy, Uncle Tim is my new dad, isn't he? And he lives here." Ellie's voice was tearful and she looked questioningly at me.

"You see," I said, taking her hands. "Time isn't the same here as on the surface. You've been here nearly a year."

"I want to talk to Mannul." Nancy's voice was full of anger and loathing. She took my rejection very hard. But I wasn't in love with her. She was just a good friend who had been married to my best friend. I thought I was helping her, as she had asked. Titch liked her, which is a bonus. But love ... no way.

"You can do that when we come back from the trip," I suggested. "Grandmother and her friend, Lex, are going to come, and the scenery will be lovely ..."

"I've seen enough!" screamed Nancy. "I'm not going on any outing."

The little girl who had come in with Ellie was standing quietly at the window. "May I come?" she asked finally, and I stooped down to her.

"Of course you may," I said. "What was your name?"

"I'm Wendy, and I'm from England," the girl answered.

She was pretty, with waist-length, dark brown hair and big, brown eyes. She had dimples in both cheeks when she smiled.

"I came here with Dad when Mummy died. He works here. I don't know how long I've been here because they say there is no time, but probably not long, anyway."

Nancy had left the room after her outburst. She returned now with a tray and four cups of the drink they have here instead of tea and coffee. She seemed to have calmed down.

"I guess I'll come," she said. "Ellie really wants to, and I might as well, as there's nothing else to do."

It was the start of an remarkable journey.

11. A Fascinating Trip

We were all seated in the one hovercraft — Grandmother, Lex, and I in front, and behind us the reluctant Nancy with Ellie at her side, a shawl and cardigan on her lap, in case it got cold. Little Wendy had clambered in beside Ellie, and the girls were giggling and whispering together, which didn't improve Nancy's mood.

Titch was sitting bolt upright between Grandmother and me. My dog was scared of nothing, but he wasn't over-confident either. Everything was new to him, and he liked everything he saw. Strangely enough, his attitude to Nancy had changed. He didn't growl or appear threatening, but he avoided her. He loved Ellie, and showed it openly and often.

We whooshed through Telos first, and when we got to the harbor the children yelled. It was a beautiful sight. Boats bobbed all around, just like in harbors everywhere, but what boats! Boats like this did not exist on the surface. They were weird shapes, and decorated like houses with chimneys, with colorful sails and loads of veils waving, in a multitude of colors and patterns. The boats themselves were painted with murals. Some looked like animals swimming: elephants, tigers, lions, turtles, dolphins, and dogs and cats. There was even a horse-boat!

I'd seen this amazing harbor before, and I asked Lex, who was at the controls, to loop around again. The wide expanse of sea stretched away from the harbor in an archipelago of islands and reefs fading into an endless blue. The girls hung over the side of the craft, crying out in delight, while Nancy held on to them, pulling them back.

"Isn't he nice?" whispered Grandmother in my ear, pointing to the back of her new admirer. I nodded and smiled. What else could I do? My grandmother was an adult who knew her own mind, and besides being a medium, she could be clear and decisive. Most people believe mediums are slightly crazy, which my grandmother had laughed at innumerable times. Actually, she was attractive for her age, rosy-hued and unwrinkled, with clear, piercing blue eyes.

As we left the magical harbor, I considered how nice it would be to walk around it with someone special. Below us was a forest with a host of different flowers. Suddenly the vehicle sank slowly downwards to land on soft, damp grass in the forest, next to a small pond and spring. Steam rose from the dark water, spreading an indescribable sense of peace. We relaxed in a ring around the hot spring. I hoped that Nancy was relaxing too. She sighed, gestured towards the spring, and said, "Hot springs aren't unusual. We have them in North America. Maybe they flow down from there."

"There's nothing quite like this on the Earth's surface," observed Lex, regarding her gravely. "Have you seen anything like this before? Look around you. Do lovely flowers like these usually grow near springs? This kind of vegetation is unique for what we can call 'the lap of the Earth.'"

"Oh, that's a lovely name!" Grandmother exclaimed, and Lex gave her an appreciative look.

"It's true," he said, smiling. "You feel that you're at the end of the world, as if the spring is a mystical entrance to another dimension."

At this juncture, a great jet spurted from the center of the spring, and everyone laughed and tried to take cover from the splashing water.

"If we all close our eyes and make a wish, it will come true," called Lex. "When there's a waterspout from the spring, you can have a wish. It's an ancient tradition here. Then we have to move on if we're going to see anything else today."

Even Nancy shut her eyes. Titch barked, and we climbed back into our hovercraft. This time, I sat next to Lex to get to know him better. He laughed and asked what I wanted to know, as the hovercraft rose, slowly negotiating the trees on the ground.

"I was born in Peru in a place where Indians have been especially persecuted by the white man," he told me. "My father was a chieftain

56

of the old order, proud and strong. I learned to ride early, so that I could accompany him on long journeys. The horse became part of me; I loved riding. It's something I miss here. My father died mysteriously, probably killed by the white governors, as he was stubborn and wouldn't do as they wished. My mother and I missed him intensely. Our tribe wanted me as chieftain, and I agreed.

"I married a wonderful woman, beautiful and wise, and we had three children — two sons and a daughter. My oldest son became chieftain after me. The younger one is studying medicine. My daughter married a boy in our tribe who is skillful and sensible. She already has four children. My wife died before our daughter got married, and I still grieve for her. It was grief that brought me here. My children are independent, and I felt lonely. I met a man from here and came back with him. It made complete sense."

"Once people are here, I can't see why they would leave this paradise," I objected.

"Some go on missions to the Earth's crust," replied Lex. "They don't stay long, and I think they select settlers viable for Telos. They are like very humane spies."

I told him about my mission to the surface and how difficult it had been to get people to accept the existence of Telos. He'd had a similar experience.

We were landing again, this time on an island. Safely and smoothly the hovercraft took us over clear, turquoise water and came in to land on soft sand. Around us were palm trees and tropical plants everywhere. Some deer came out from the trees, approaching us cautiously.

"They're used to people," remarked Lex. "This is a zoo of sorts. I thought it would be fun for the girls. All the animals here are more or less tame and completely safe, even the lions and bears, those kings of the forest. They don't hunt each other or man. And, we actually have dragons here."

"Dragons!" exclaimed the girls in chorus. "Aren't dragons only in stories?"

"Of course not!" I objected. "They just don't want to live near bloodthirsty people any more. They want to live in peace. Dragons are wonderful animals."

I'd only seen one dragon in Telos, fairly soon after I first came. I told the girls, who were ready for stories, that dragons were neither myth nor legend. They were real animals which had roamed the Earth thousands of years ago. There had also been real dragon-riders. Often young boys chose the job, as the training was long and they had to be supple and fit to succeed. Dragons had taken refuge in Agartha when humans began to hunt and kill more and more of them. They had stayed and made their home up here in the wild mountains of Agartha. Some of them were tame and used as transport.

Dragons are beautiful, and glint in a multitude of colors, but basically they are as dark green as the forest. People here have invented secure saddles, and hold riding classes. Dragons are acknowledged to be at least as intelligent as horses, and have learned respect for the inhabitants of Telos. The dragon I met was testing out an inexperienced rider.

The girls were overjoyed, and Nancy was listening, although I could tell from her expression that she didn't believe me. Lex backed me up, telling us of the dragons he had seen and one that he had ridden briefly. He also told us of other wild animals which had died out on the surface of the Earth, but which existed inside the Earth.

"Have you noticed how lovely it smells here?" exclaimed my grandmother in delight. I hadn't thought of it, as I'm used to the smell of all the beautiful flowers. Now I noticed something aromatic, and Lex explained.

"On this island they grow exotic spices, which grow wild among the other plants here. They don't usually plant seeds in beds, but strew them in the wild and allow them to spread, to be picked when needed. We're going to visit one of the growers."

The growers lived in round, roofless houses, which are standard here. There was a fence around each house. Lex explained that this was because the animals were inquisitive sometimes, and it was deemed unnecessary to have lions or bears trampling around the children.

We stopped outside a house where the owners were taking a break. We were invited in and given the tea-like drink which is consumed instead of coffee, and bread instead of cakes. Afterwards, we saw the plantation, which was a jumble of plant-life, where everything which grew was allowed space. There was no question of weeding, as the weeds were cared for in the same way as the other plants. The farmer strode around his property with a musical instrument. He sang and played the whole time. He played a guitar, and his children played flutes beautifully. Nancy put her hands to her ears and asked them to stop, which made Grandmother cross.

"If you can't behave nicely, you might as well go home," she said severely. "The music is lovely, and the rest of us are enjoying it. Look at your daughter!" Ellie and Wendy were dancing merrily on the grass, singing and laughing until the tears rolled down their rosy cheeks.

We saw wild animals, too. First a bear trotted up. When he saw us he reared up on his hind legs. Lex went and patted his chest. The bear sniffed at him, enjoying the attention. When it was back down on all fours and Lex was still stroking it, Grandmother and I joined him. The bear was just as sweet as it should be, I thought. But we hadn't reckoned on Titch.

Titch was sitting nicely with the children, who hung back, obviously scared. He had decided to protect the little girls. He didn't like the smell of bear, and he growled when the bear was back on all fours. Lex whispered something into the bear's ear just as it was beginning to snarl. It turned around and loped off towards the forest.

"I think we should move on," Lex decided. "Otherwise there could be more of the same, which might scare the girls. I can come back another day with Tim and Emilie."

12. A Real Live Dragon!

The more you see of Agartha, the more you wonder that the outer and inner Earths exist in such close proximity to one another. There are similarities and differences: differences in the buildings and infrastructure; similarities in the scenery. Next time the hovercraft stopped, it was in front of quite a large, round building with a hatch on the front. I pressed a button near the door. A friendly face appeared in the opening.

"What do you want to eat?" I asked. "We're at a food bar and we can order vegetarian food here."

There were tables and chairs among the pots of plants outside. The children crowded forward. The friendly-face person showed them pictures of what they could order. Laughing cheerfully, the girls pointed to what they wanted, and I helped the others order. Nancy wasn't hungry, and just wanted a glass of water. The rest of us enjoyed attractive meals served in the flower garden.

This was the most common kind of bar or restaurant in Telos. The food was prepared in the large, round house and distributed from there.

"Let's get on!" called Lex when we'd all finished eating. The hovercraft was nearby. No parking problems here, as it didn't touch the ground. I was lifting up Ellie under her arms when Nancy stopped me.

"I want to go home," she demanded. "I've got a terrible headache. Ellie's coming with me." Ellie begged and begged, but Nancy was firm. I arranged another vehicle for them and programmed in Nancy's address, but Wendy wouldn't go with them. Ellie, devastated, waved until she could see us no longer.

"What a hard-hearted mother," remarked Grandmother crossly. "Little Ellie is a nice child, and we could easily have looked after her."

"Nancy is probably one of the most normal people ever," Lex observed. "People who are thoroughly normal can't cope with the atmosphere here. Unfortunately, it's probably best for her to go home." I nodded in agreement.

I felt a small hand in mine, and a lock of gleaming, dark hair brushed my hand as I was getting into our transport. "Can I sit with you?" the child asked, and I smiled and nodded.

Suddenly, the hovercraft dipped earthwards with unusual rapidity. The woodland here was less dense, with moss and flowers on the ground. We drew up beside a mountain with a cave. With a finger on his lips, Lex waved us out of the vehicle. He led us to a camouflaged shelter where there were clumps of grass to sit on. Sitting quietly, we wondered what was going on. We soon found out!

The first thing we saw was smoke coming from the cave, followed by huge smoky nostrils, and a shiny green head with large eyes and tiny ears. Soon a whole dragon had appeared, its tail swishing the ground. Beside it was a small dragon with less intense coloring, presumably a baby.

I put my hand to Wendy's mouth to keep her from screaming. She stared, and then buried her head in my shoulder. Grandmother and Lex were holding hands, watching the unusual creatures in delight. I was glad Nancy wasn't with us. She would have been terrified. Titch didn't even growl. He sat at my side as though turned to stone, staring.

I'm not really used to children, and I didn't notice until it was too late that Wendy had crept up to the dragon. Frozen in horror, I watched her put out her hand to stroke its nose. Wendy's entire being seemed to emanate Love. Grandmother and Lex got ready to rescue her.

To our surprise, the dragon stuck out a long, pink tongue and gave Wendy a wet, steamy lick on the face. Then the dragon shook its huge body, checked that the baby dragon was close (it was definitely a dragon mother), and spread its enormous wings, while the baby dragon did the same. They rose slowly and majestically, flapping their wings in farewell. The adult dragon turned her head and gave us a long, keen look. My grandmother nearly fainted as she dried her tears, laughing in relief.

Wendy stood watching the amazing animals until Lex took her hand.

"Come on, little one, let's go," he said.

Wendy ran up and hugged me. "It was grrreat" she exclaimed. "I'm going to tell my mum and dad all about it."

Puzzled, I looked at her. Mum? I wondered. I knew she was dead.

"I quite often talk to Mum," she declared happily, pointing to her heart. "She's inside me, and she always answers."

I'd thought that Ellie was an amazing child, but here was another one. Maybe there are plenty of amazing children, but I'm not used to meeting them.

With Wendy chattering happily at my side, I alighted from the hovercraft at the next stop. Grandmother and Lex were heading straight for something that looked like an aircraft hangar, which is exactly what it turned out to be. I knew Agartha was extensive, but I hadn't really understood quite how extensive.

This was a transport station for hovercraft of various sorts. It wasn't bleak and noisy and full of brash travelers weighed down with luggage, like our mainline stations. There were tunnels here reaching across the inner Earth and right up to the outside. These crossed Agartha, as well as the planet's crust. The tunnels had existed for many thousands of years. You could go nearly anywhere in the small, covered vehicles which were parked in rows. As usual, Grandmother clapped her hands in surprise and wonder as Lex reeled off facts about the amazing Central Station.

Wendy asked, "Uncle Tim, do you think I could go and visit Mum from here?"

"She doesn't really live in these parts," I objected, upset. "To get to her, you need a special sort of plane which they don't have here. You can't visit the dead, Wendy. You can only be sure that they are alive and well in another dimension. But you have her image within you, like you said, and that is lovely."

"I'll have to wait until I'm big," sighed Wendy. "Anyway, I can see elementals, as Dad calls them. I usually tell him that I have tiny friends who are sometimes quite see-through. Some of them have pointed hats and some have hair like sunshine and small, transparent wings pretty much like bumble-bees."

"Can you see them here?" Grandmother asked.

"Of course, and we talk about everything!" Wendy's eyes widened. "Is there something wrong with that?"

"Not in the least. You are very lucky!" Grandmother stroked the dark hair of this wonderful child.

"I think we've seen enough for today!" exclaimed Lex, and we clambered back into the hovercraft with Titch beside me as lookout.

Now I understood the dragon's behavior. Wendy was more elemental than human, although she looked human enough as she curled up close and rested her head on my shoulder. She was sleeping soundly, sucking her thumb, by the time we got home.

I carried the sleeping child into Grandmother's house. Lex disappeared momentarily, returning with the news that he'd contacted Wendy's father, who would soon collect his daughter. I knew that the contact had been telepathic, but Grandmother was confused.

"I thought that phones were on the surface of the planet," she said.

"We've got a good one in our heads," I teased, because she already knew that.

Grandmother smiled and asked me to open the door, just as a loud knocking was heard. A dark, slightly stocky man entered. He grinned amiably and said, "I'm Wendy's dad, Edmund. Have you got my charming monkey here?"

Behind him appeared a countenance which could only belong to a small, mischievous boy. "This is my nephew, Wendy's cousin," continued Edmund. "He arrived today, and was disappointed to find his cousin was out. He's called Pierre. He's nine, and has come because his parents died in a car crash. I'm going to take care of him."

"Wendy is welcome to come as often as she wants, such a sweet child," my grandmother interrupted, "and the lad too, by the way. I like children and can always find something interesting to do. Please sit down, and my grandson will fetch the lass."

I returned with the child, who was still fast asleep. She opened her eyes briefly and mumbled, "Dad!" and then slumbered again. Pierre stayed calmly behind his uncle, watching his sleeping cousin in amazement.

Children can sleep safely even thousands of feet inside the Earth, in a brilliant kingdom called Agartha.

13. Nancy and Ellie Return Home

Mannul was waiting in the arbor at my house. The slight dampness in the pale night air intensified the scent of flowers.

I got us hot drinks and biscuits and we sat down comfortably. Titch laid his great head in Mannul's lap. I realized this was a great honor.

"Now you've met other surface-dwellers who have come here and want to stay," began the man with the long, nearly-white hair. "Just like you, they have had certain experiences which have brought them here. People from Earth don't end up here by accident. It wasn't by accident that your ship went down and you were saved. Neither was it an accident that Lex came to us; he had known about us for a long time.

"However, Nancy isn't particularly welcome. We knew she wouldn't fit in here, but we gave her a chance because she is your friend. It hasn't gone well. I have talked to her, and she's returning to the surface via Mount Shasta tomorrow. We'll provide financial help, as she couldn't get home otherwise."

"It's not what Ellie wants," I sighed. "But she can always return when she's older, if she doesn't forget us."

"We've decided it's your duty to go with them, Tim." I guess I looked far from delighted, for he began laughing.

"You only need put them on the first flight to Seattle. Then you can return immediately, if you're not tempted to stay a while on Earth, that is." I shook my head firmly, and he laughed again.

"We'll wake you in plenty of time tomorrow. Go to Nancy's and there will be a hovercraft there. Nancy will be taking precious stones with her, so she'll manage financially. Arniel wants to see you as soon as you get back, so contact me at once. Have a good trip!" With a smile, he hugged me and disappeared out the door. When I looked around, he was gone.

In the morning I was awakened by a small bird chirruping like a canary on my shoulder. I got dressed and hurried to Nancy's house.

Nancy was sitting outside on her suitcase, and Ellie was on the grass, tears streaming down her face. Titch sat down beside the girl and looked as if he was trying to comfort her. She buried her head in his huge doggy neck. I lifted her gently into the hovercraft. Nancy inclined her head slightly in my direction and asked, "Are you coming with us?"

"Only as far as the plane."

She got into the vehicle, and I sat in front. She avoided looking at me, and I hoped the whole journey would be over quickly.

"I had expected you to be more honorable," remarked Nancy. "I never believed my husband's best friend would be so unreliable."

Honestly, I was astonished. "How am I unreliable?" I asked.

"First you came on to me and then, as soon as we came here, you cast me aside for that blond tart. You know, that woman you danced with. I was brought here under false pretenses. I feel betrayed. This isn't paradise. It's just the opposite!"

"You'll probably find you brought that with you," I retorted, suppressing my anger. "Haven't you learned the seven virtues which I've repeated to you every day? We live by them in this country."

"Appreciation, Compassion, Forgiveness, Humility, Understanding, Valor, and Unconditional Love, of course!" Ellie came out with this line. I thought she'd drifted off next to Titch. My dog made a "talking" noise, one of those dog-mumbles which most dog-owners would recognize.

"And that doesn't include jealousy," I added, "especially as I've never encouraged you. That was your interpretation."

Nancy didn't have time to reply, because the craft landed at the enormous station I described earlier. We drove along a track into a tunnel. Ellie put her arms around Titch, but he was sitting bolt upright, staring into the darkness. There were small, weak lamps on the tunnel walls, and I could see Nancy's rigid face, her mouth drooping. Then she put her hand on my arm.

"Can't you forgive me so things will be like they were before?" she asked. "Then I can come and visit you sometime. I'm rich now, thanks to your generous friends."

"Getting back here won't be as easy as you think," I replied grimly. "You were here thanks to me, and won't be able to return unless I wish it. That's how it works."

Nancy was silent for the rest of the journey, while Ellie chattered about all her experiences. But she was happy to be getting home to their old house and her friends. They would never believe her stories. As we got out of the hovercraft, she chirruped, "Soon I'll be able to ring Garth and Linny and Polly and Ann on our phone. And Mum will drive us on trips in the summer ..."

The heavy gate reverberated with a hollow clang behind us as we climbed the stairway to Mount Shasta. Outside, in the parking lot, was a taxi. The driver approached and called out my name. The taxi was pre-booked and would drive us straight to the airport. We got in.

I'll never forget Nancy's last words to me. I held out my hand and was going to give her a friendly hug, but she pulled away and stood on the bottom step to the airplane.

"I hate you, Tim," she declared gravely. "I'm going to get my revenge and really hurt you. I'm going to do my best to stop Ellie ever returning here. I despise you, Timothy."

I didn't believe Nancy for a moment. She had a quick temper. But it didn't feel good. I reached down and patted big Titch on the head. He licked my hand and I felt better at once. Dogs aren't just our best friends, they're more than that. They are our conscience, good or bad, and they lick away our troubles before they can grow worse, and their loyal faces bring us strength and courage.

Titch and I returned to Telos without any further trouble, and I went straight to Grandmother's house. Lex was there, of course, and Edmund, while Wendy and her cousin Pierre were chasing each other in the beautiful, little garden. It was lovely and restful hearing happy children and joyful laughter. Titch went off to join in at once.

Lex laughed when he heard about my disagreeable leave-taking from Nancy. "Don't worry about that woman; she can't hurt you here, Tim," he said. "Forgive her, and pray that she gets the help she needs. Let go of all your thoughts about her. Transmit light and Love to replace the bad. Remember that evil can't survive light, so transmit plenty of light."

I already know all of this, but it never hurts to be reminded of good things, of the proximity of the Great Light. We Earthlings find this easy to forget.

When I returned home, Arniel and Mannul were waiting in the little arbor in my garden. I didn't bother to tell them about Nancy; I realized they already knew.

"Forget Nancy and the surface and all the unpleasant things you have experienced," said Arniel. "We have other tidings. First, you are going on a trip with your grandmother and the others, and Mannul is going with you as guide. It will be quite a long journey, because you need to know more about our land if you are going to stay here. It will be good for the children, too. Ellie ought to have stayed, as we need gifted children like her. But I think she will return, and maybe you will have to collect her, Tim. But that is for the future.

"When this trip is over, we would like you to operate as a bridge between the surface and here. You will be informed later what this will involve. But I can promise you plenty of exciting and instructive adventures. You will meet many people because you have much of the Earthling still in you, which we need to preserve, as it is so positive. There is an acquaintance you will be making soon which will be especially important and instructive for all of us."

14. Meeting Saint Germain

We were back in a hovercraft: Mannul, Grandmother, and I, with Titch, Lex, Wendy, Edmund, and Pierre. Only Lex knew where we were going. In actual fact, Grandmother and I knew very little about Agartha as a country and Telos as a town. We hadn't had much time to be tourists. Mannul turned to smile at me, while the children pretended to be scared as we reached hover height, which seemed to be just above the trees at the moment. Sometimes, hover height was a few inches above the ground, but apparently we were going further, so the hovercraft flew like an aircraft. We were tightly strapped in, luckily. I shared with the children my feeling that this was an enchanted journey, and they loved the idea.

There were huge birds flying in formation, well away from us. Smaller birds flew around us, chirruping all the time. Finally, we were coming down. Fear gave way to excitement. Where were we?

We landed in lush, green, fairly tall grass, which grows all over Agartha. Mannul jumped out quickly and offered a gentlemanly hand to my grandmother before the other men got out. I looked around. Was it a South Sea island? There were palms all around, between which we glimpsed a sea as blue as the Mediterranean.

"We're going to meet someone here," Mannul remarked. "He and I are going to divide you between us and guide you around. He's visiting Agartha and has been here a while. He's from another dimension, but has asked to come here, much for the sake of Mariana, the medium who Tim will be in contact with. Look, here he is!"

A tall, elegant man approached rapidly from a palm grove. I recognized his happy, open face, but I couldn't think why. He came up to me, took both my hands, smiled with sparkling teeth, and embraced me. Then he hugged the other men. Imagine my surprise when he kissed Grandmother's hand! She looked delighted. He crouched down to joke with the children, and even Titch was patted thoroughly without any objections. The dog licked him as if he was an old friend.

"I recognize you," observed Grandmother, regarding him with a raised eyebrow. "Are you an author, or an actor? Are you British or Swedish?"

"None of those," he replied with a smile. "I'm Saint Germain, and I visit Agartha occasionally. They call me Master. I come from the stars, and was incarnated on Earth as a spiritual teacher, long before Jesus Christ. I made appearances in France in the reign of Louis XIV. I'm a spiritual leader to many who live now, and here is one of my loyal pupils, as large as life, this little lady who is asking who I am."

"Grandmother!" I exclaimed.

Mannul took the newcomer aside and appeared to receive instructions. Then, with a wave and a bow, Mannul disappeared. The great Master returned to us.

"I know where we're going now," he commented. "We'll take the hovercraft a little further."

In this part of the planet, there are obviously long distances, but there are also ways and means of shortening them. The hovercraft seemed to have a variety of speeds, and now it raced forward a few inches from the ground.

When it stopped, the landscape had completely changed. We were at the foot of a fire-spewing volcano. The fire didn't pour downwards, but instead disappeared upwards into a dark cloud. At the great foot of the volcano was a village. There were the typical Agarthan buildings: round, roofless houses surrounded by luxuriant vegetation.

Grandmother clasped her hands together, as was her habit, and cried, "How splendid! How impressive! How can they build so close to a volcano? Imagine if there was an eruption, like Vesuvius!"

Lex guffawed. "Emilie, dearest, this is Vesuvius! At least, that's what it's called on the surface, and we are just beneath Italy. Volcanoes erupt upwards here, not downwards!"

Grandmother stared at him. "How do you know these things, Lex?" she wondered, and the rest of us burst out laughing. Then we turned around to watch the amazing sight.

"I thought you were considered a magician, as there was no corpse in your coffin, but you seem very much alive," I remarked to Saint Germain. He laughed heartily.

"Where I come from, you can appear in various guises, as necessary," he replied. "That is possible here, too, but not in Telos, another part of Agartha. The fifth dimension is in ascendancy there, invisible to humans. This region has much ancient wisdom and history, which I'm interested in. I like gadding about in ancient history. I feel oddly at home in it. But let's continue with this tour."

Just then, we heard a scream, followed by another scream. Wendy was running towards us. "Pierre has drowned in the volcano!" she screamed. "He's all sooty!"

It was our turn to run now. The Master, with his long legs, arrived first, to find an amorphous blob of coal-dust, spitting and hissing like an angry cat. It was not a laughing matter, but it was very comical.

"Pierre was trying to balance on the edge over there," Wendy explained. "Then he slipped, and I had to pull him out, and Titch helped. He took Pierre's pullover in his teeth and pulled!"

My handsome dog turned up covered in soot too. Saint Germain took over now. "This is something I have learned down the eons of time!" he said, standing in front of the mucky boy and the sputtering dog. Titch's coat was black anyway, so now it was difficult to see where the soot ended and his nose began.

The ancient Master was before them, raising his hands and muttering. A black cloud lifted from the child and the dog. It disappeared into the sky, leaving the boy and dog to be hugged by everyone. Wendy was at my side, holding my hand.

"I should've rolled in it too," she said thoughtfully. "Then I would've got lots of hugs too." I gave her a huge bear-hug in reply.

We continued in the hovercraft. "So you come from heaven?" I smiled at the interesting newcomer. He smiled back.

"I don't think you really know who I am. My mission is to visit the three-dimensional part of Agartha, temporarily, from the five-dimensional part. Our new inhabitants, yourself included, Tim, must be incorporated easily with our original inhabitants. You people in this hovercraft constitute newcomers, as there are great swathes of our continent you are not yet familiar with. The children will learn about it in school, but you must experience the country naturally.

"I have lived in and visited other dimensions before settling where I am. Telos is part of the area I am responsible for, though there are many others. There are plenty of wise Masters here, but I am in charge of movement and organization for innovation. In Telos I have a physical body, but not in the other areas of Agartha. Now, let's get to know the outskirts of Telos."

The hovercraft was coming down.

A massive, round building caught our attention. There was a soft humming in the air, as if from a thousand bumblebees. Turning around, we found a similar building behind us, and one to either side. We were ringed by massive, roofless buildings.

"A lot of manufacturing takes place here!" called Lex. "We make food and drink in one of these buildings, furniture and interior products in another. These are businesses you have on the surface in a different form. The children might be interested in the sweets. Run through that green door there, Wendy and Pierre, and someone will look after you!"

The children didn't need to be told twice; they disappeared immediately through the green door. The rest of us, including Titch, were taken on a voyage of discovery we won't forget for a long time. Everything was made by hand or using very simple tools, not machines. There was a holy heap of stuff, implements of all kinds. When we emerged from the building, the children were waiting by the hovercraft, chewing and sucking, obviously pleased with themselves.

We were incredibly impressed and surprised at the variety of things which could be produced without machinery.

"I have been an escapist all of my life, and have been seeking only the search itself," declared my petite grandmother as we sat down in our unique vehicle. "I'm glad the search is over. This is where I want to grow old."

"You won't grow old here; you'll get younger," explained Saint Germain. "Aging is an above-Earth process, and actually completely unnecessary. Look at Tim. He's been here for many Earth years, and still looks just as he did when he first came. This is how it will be with you, too. Much has been written of my youthful appearance, which never seemed to age. I live a wholesome life here, and know about youth and health. The children have to grow up first, but we can help Emilie and the men to become younger. There are houses like the ones you see here, which offer various treatments for visitors who decide to stay."

We continued our strange journey.

15. Magical Buildings

It was lunchtime, or perhaps dinnertime. As time didn't exist and the sun wasn't like the one on Earth, it was difficult to determine anything, except that our stomachs were rumbling.

Lex took us in to land in a village outside Telos, near a café. We sat down, and after making sure the hungry children had food, ordered some for us.

"How do we pay? I haven't seen anyone produce a wallet since we came. No notes, no coins?" It was Grandmother who pointed this out.

"Here payment is different," began Lex.

"In kind?" Grandmother interrupted, eyes glittering with lurking laughter. "I'm too old for that!"

"Grandmother!" I remonstrated. "There's no money on Telos, just service. We provide for each other, exchange goods, and waste nothing. There are collection areas for exchange, instead of shops. It's well-organized, as you will see."

Grandmother was visibly enjoying a delicious cake. The children were cramming in everything on offer.

"Food is necessary for survival," Saint Germain smiled and said. "It's provided in Agartha."

"On the surface, nothing is provided without payment," remarked Edmund. "That kind of difference is like chalk and cheese."

We continued our hovercraft journey into the unknown.

Next time we landed, we were taken by surprise. We were on a mountainside, near an amazing building. It was more oval than round, and glittered with precious stones. It had a greenish glow: "The Jade Temple," explained Saint Germain.

It wasn't in any particular style, this temple. It was like a fairy-tale castle with towers and pinnacles, more decorative afterthoughts than necessities. It was very beautiful.

"You have churches," he commented as we alighted. "We have buildings for meditation. You can enjoy a moment of contemplation whenever you wish. Let's go in."

We were so fascinated by the exterior of the temple that it was difficult to drag ourselves away to go inside. It was unlike anything we had seen before, glinting and gleaming as if alive.

"I've always been interested in UFOs," declared Edmund, who had previously said very little. "This reminds me of an inverted UFO somehow. It's how you would imagine another planet, and yet we're still here on Earth. It's very weird."

"There are plenty of weird things here!" observed Lex cheerfully, gesturing for us to enter the magnificent, jewel-studded door. The pearly gate, I thought, smiling.

Inside was exquisite. The precious stones covering the walls cast a dull, shimmering gleam across the hall. There were plenty of comfortable couches and chairs upholstered in a velvet-like material. People were sitting, lost in meditation, or just resting, and we found our way to two sofas facing each other.

The children realized they had to be calm and quiet, and seemed bewitched. They sat with their eyes closed and hands clasped. I knew these buildings were known as "Houses of God's Love" and were thousands of years old. There was something magical about them which words can't express.

Music was playing softly and there was something aromatic which intensified the atmosphere, rather than otherwise. I shut my eyes and lost myself in it.

It wasn't long before a man and woman were standing in the middle of the room. They talked to us telepathically. There were no voices, but they talked in turn, clearly, in our heads. They both were tall and well-built. The woman's hair was long and fair, the man's long and raven-black. They were dressed in kaftan-like robes with glittering edging and embroidery, the woman in pink and the man in green.

"Welcome to the House of God's Love," said the man, in English, at least that's the language I heard. "In this haven of tranquility, your thoughts can cease their frantic dance and you can allow feelings and impressions to take over. It's time to look inwards at who you are."

"You may not be who you think you are!" the clear female voice declared. "Be honest with yourselves.

"You children will find a story and sweets waiting behind the curtain over there." The children disappeared at once. The telepathic speech continued with the male voice.

"You are newcomers, and very welcome! I want to explain some special attributes of the area of Mother Earth where you are now. If you still believe that the Earth is solid and you're dreaming, I can relieve you of your delusion. Both the North and South Poles converge in an enormous inner cavity with its own sun and beautiful surroundings, where people can live in great well-being with an ancient culture."

"Our capital city is Shamballa," the female voice took up the tale. "It's in the center of the planet. Our energy is free and inexhaustible. Our inhabitants travel by hovercraft, as you have done, because we wish to conserve Nature and allow it to grow naturally. A tunnel system across the whole planet has formed a well-planned communications network for centuries. Energy comes from crystals hooked up to electromagnetism, which will last five hundred thousand years."

"The Earth's crust is approximately 800 miles (1 300 km) thick," the man continued. "The magnetic field of Earth has always been a mystery to scientists on the surface. Our inner sun in the center of the Earth is the mysterious power source which generates the magnetic field around our planet."

"Nowadays, there are entrances to Agartha across the whole planet," interrupted the woman, laughing. "We can stay in contact, as long as you know we exist. We know you do, anyway. There was an entrance in the Library of Alexandria, which burned down in 47 BCE. There are millions of us here, but in the last 200 years we have only accepted 50 people from the surface."

The man added, "You have visited our immense library, Porthologos, albeit somewhat briefly. It is actually under the Aegean Sea. It is enchanted, literally. It is the seat of learning, a world university, the stronghold of magic, a center for the Arts and much, much more. A surface lifetime would not give you enough time to research all its secrets, but we live for hundreds of years, so we get more opportunity to study them."

"You're interested in our inhabitants, aren't you?" the woman asked, and we nodded. "We are similar to you, but taller. Good food and fine thoughts keep us youthful and extend our lives. We have been vegetarians for 12,000 years. This is good for our figures. We'll teach you. We are planning to come to the surface and offer help. The schedule is not definite yet, but your need grows more urgent. We already have informers up there."

"We could carry on for hours," observed the man. "But we're not going to. We want you to experience our vast continent for yourselves, not by reading about it, or flying through it briefly. You ought to know in advance that Telos and its district are the only part where surface-dwellers feel really at home. There are huge unexplored forests, fields, mountains, and seas that cover great parts of Agartha. You'll recognize much of the flora and fauna.

"We have many towns which are five-dimensional, which you'll have to learn before you can go there. You'll spend plenty of time in Porthologos, and will travel around, too. As the newest group from the surface, we would like you all to study Agartha together. We are honored that our respected friend and Master, Saint Germain, is with you, and we will do all we can to ensure you have a comfortable journey."

"You can take the lift from here to Porthologos," the woman informed us. "Lex will show you the way. You'll need to take the children with you, as there is a kind of school where they can stay and learn, while you explore Agartha. The practicalities of your trip are all arranged. What you learn from it is up to each of you individually."

"Will it be dangerous?" my grandmother asked delicately.

"You may sometimes experience danger, but remaining positive and transmitting Love and happiness will protect you. You may meet life-forms that you don't recognize and elementals who know nothing of life on the surface. Fear is unacceptable. You must suppress your fear and even your anger, unless it is just. You'll see what I mean." The man nodded and smiled.

"We're only here to prepare you. Nobody can come and live here without being tested. We dare not take any risks with people from the surface. However, most people who don't fit in realize it themselves, and decide not to stay. Tim is already one of us, but you could say that he's sanctioning his citizenship by accompanying Emilie, Lex, and Edmund. The Master travels where he wants, and you might need him.

"So there you are! Your new life starts now!"

82

16. Shamballa —
A Paradise Inside the Earth

Our new life started with some time at home, as we Earthlings still needed to sleep at night. The next "morning," we met at my house to decide where we would go. We found that everything had been arranged, and all we had to do was to sit in the remote-controlled hovercraft. It was pre-programmed. And there was a big surprise. Mannul knocked on my door early.

"I have your guide with me," he remarked. "Tim, you know Telos well, but this guide knows the whole of Agartha."

A grinning young woman appeared. It was Sisilla!

"I hope you don't mind if I'm your guide." She smiled calmly and held out her hand, which I took. It felt like a butterfly wing in my earthly paw, and I shivered with happiness.

Outside, the members of our small group had gathered. Grandmother hugged Sisilla, who welcomed her. Edmund and Lex stared in surprise and delight. Sisilla looked like a fairy-tale princess, dressed in a long robe in shades of blue, with a wide, sparkling silver belt. Her long, silvery-blond hair was tied high on her head, with curling strands falling to her neck. She was preternaturally beautiful.

"I will explain each place in your own language," she said, in fluent English. "Please get into the hovercraft!"

"What about the children?" exclaimed Grandmother.

"They were taken asleep to the place in Porthologos where they will stay. Rest assured, they will be fed and watered, and there will be no lack of games, songs, dancing, and stories for them."

Titch, big and black, was calm at my side, his gaze on our fair guide.

She laughed, bent down, and whispered in his ear, stroking him on the neck. He answered with a typical Titch-sigh and licked her hand. Then he lay down, awaiting my command.

There was room for all of us in the vehicle. It was comfortable, with cushioned seats and safety conveniences. Sisilla sat next to Grandmother, and I had to be content with Titch as my partner. We took off, gently and slowly at first, above the roofless houses, and then over a foaming sea, with the distant horizon as our only view. Grandmother and Sisilla talked eagerly together, while Titch and I slumbered. I only hope I didn't snore as loudly as he did!

The distant horizon approached rapidly, and soon we could distinguish lush vegetation in a wide band across the strip of land we were passing. We came in to land in the middle of all the greenery. Titch, still hazy with sleep, sat up and growled. He has a special growl, ending in a yelp, which I like to think is an expression of contentment. There were plenty of trees here, and he jumped out of the hovercraft in a kangaroo bound as soon as I released him from the safety harness.

"There are numerous groves of trees in this country which are landing places," Sisilla told us. "They all lead somewhere, so we're going to see where this one leads!"

She led us through the wood to a gate constructed from boughs and branches. It was amazingly lovely, and I wondered that we didn't make things like that on Earth. It was tall, and bent in various patterns, the green leaves still on some branches. The fence it was set in was in a similar style, and just as beautiful. Sisilla opened the gate by pressing a rose in the pattern. Behind it was a lightly-trodden path.

"We're beyond Telos now," announced our guide. "You may not know that our country is studded with jewel-towns, as their foundations are gold and precious stones.

"Down the ages, further back than you can imagine, we have mined and used the riches of the rocks. This humble path leads to our capital city, Shamballa! The place has played many roles in history. It is allegedly in the Gobi Desert, in another dimension, in heaven, and only a figment of your imagination. It's actually here, and in a moment you'll see the real, genuine, and at least partly physical Shamballa."

The dense forest and unassuming path disappeared. It was as if a massive curtain had been drawn from our eyes. A glittering, shimmering, sparkling town was laid out in front of us. Shamballa! The name itself caused shivers of delight and respect.

"Shamballa!" exclaimed Grandmother, with worship in her eyes. "Where the streets are of gold, the houses of marble, and symphonies are playing. Where there are beautiful people clad in white, and there is the high-seat of the great Masters. Do you mean that we're really there?"

"We are!" boomed Saint Germain's happy voice. He wasn't with us in the hovercraft, so I don't know where he came from. "You'll soon see, Emilie! I know this town well. Paris doesn't compare!"

He had hardly finished speaking when we felt firm ground beneath our feet. Grandmother's exclamation was no exaggeration: We were walking on a golden street. But our feet didn't touch the gold ingots. We hovered a little above them. Our steps became a smooth glide forward. We followed Sisilla, having no idea where she would lead us.

Each house we passed was a poem, a temple. I have never seen such beautiful buildings before. We were bathed in a lovely, silvery light. We stopped by a tall structure, more of an enchanted castle than a house. It was set slightly apart, surrounded by an incredible garden. Earthly eyes would hardly call this a town with houses; it was more like paradise.

"I thought I'd seen everything," declared Lex slowly, "but this exceeds EVERYTHING."

Light, shimmering halls, singing, smiling people dressed in pale colors, wise men with halos, the interplay of colors on the walls, dancing children, and heavenly music in the background. What more can be said of the ineffable? Shamballa is no exaggeration. It is exactly how we dream the seat of peace and love to be.

I thought Sisilla took us away too quickly, but we had a glimpse of all that is the paradise of Shamballa, in its rightful place. It was partly Earth-like and partly unearthly.

There was something fragile about these people who were not as firmly-fleshed as us. There were huge variations, and some were hardly human, except in form. Shamballa is a vast place, with many races and different types of beings. They all had one thing in common: Love of the Highest Source and of others. The power of Love flowed through this palace, filling our hearts with such happiness that it nearly hurt.

I glanced at Sisilla, and she returned my look. In that moment, the Love between us, which had kept a discreet distance, finally came to the fore. She came to me, and I embraced her. She rested her head against my shoulder as Grandmother turned and smiled. We were quiet for a long time. It was time to leave this amazing building. An oratorio from the 17th century resonated around us as we left the hall.

Titch ran around wildly when we emerged. He had been quiet inside, lying at my feet. Now he careened around madly, with people laughing and shrieking as he bounded past them. We met other dogs, although, weirdly enough, Titch didn't seem to see them. Usually, he liked to touch other dogs, but now it was as though they didn't exist.

"Are they ghost dogs?" I asked, as a bunch of Dalmatians stopped to greet him. Titch walked right through the spotted dogs. That was the answer to my question.

"Some earthly dogs arrive here in non-physical form," Saint Germain told us. "This place has five dimensions, and you can't expect normality here. Outside Telos, most of Agartha is five-dimensional. If you don't mind, I will be narrator for a while. I'm going to recount the story of how I came here. I think it might interest our readers."

My attention at this juncture was on our beautiful guide, so it was great that he took over. He was more used to an audience than me.

17. An Exciting Encounter with Wild Animals

"I was in the place I usually stay when I'm not on Earth," Saint Germain said, "when I was called to a higher place.

"'It's time for Agartha to be revealed to humankind above Earth,' one of the Masters declared to me, 'and the task falls to you.'

"Invisible or visible?" I ventured to ask. He laughed.

"'In this case, you have the pleasure of being either, as it suits you. You are to convey the secrets of Agartha to three-dimensional people who have just come and want to stay. They will change to five dimensions when they are ready. The whole Earth must change.'

"Change has been needed for a long time, when you consider the 21st century," I replied. "Even earlier, when I think of the disasters invented in the elegant period I was part of."

"But now I'm here to help the surface Earthlings, when these huge revolutionary changes come into force on the Earth."

"Are you looking forward to the Great Light?" wondered Emilie. "Or have you already been there?"

"Not in the way you're thinking." Saint Germain smiled. "I have too much left of our beloved Earth in me, so I'm used as an intermediary between various dimensions and times. But now we have to move on. We're going to visit the Great Chasm. Nature without parallel."

It was good to have Saint Germain with us. I wasn't worried about dangerous adventures or hostile peoples, as the concept of hostile didn't exist here. But I was on my own voyage of exploration: Sisilla. It was time for me to settle down in this corner of the world and find my life-partner. I had done this, but I needed to know that she agreed.

Maybe this was a starting point, not a tourist trip. Sisilla turned as if she'd heard my thoughts, and smiled in a way that gave me great hope. Grandmother caught our smiles and looked away.

The Great Chasm really was gigantic. We struggled out of the hovercraft and stood dumbfounded. It was just as well there was a fence to stop us from rushing forward. How far back it went, or how deep it was, I have no idea, but Sisilla took over. The fence was iron, wrought in a strange pattern, with a gate. Sisilla stood before it.

"In the Great Chasm lives a people who are completely unknown to you. They have been here since the dawn of time, and will probably remain forever. They are giants from ancient times and can be thirteen to sixteen feet (four to five meters) tall, and are heavily built. To modern eyes, they wear strange skins almost like Vikings. But they are not warriors. They work as we do, with positive energies, love, happiness, dance, and music.

"Unfortunately, they are extremely shy and dislike visitors.

"The Great Chasm is a kingdom in its own right. They have their own culture, and are not influenced by others who live here. A path runs down the chasm and a tunnel leads into their kingdom. Inside are the same sky and heavenly bodies that we have. They share our sun and their air is as pure as ours. They are farmers. A point of interest is that they have dairy cattle on their farms. These are similar to the cows you have on the surface, but bigger and a different color."

While she was talking, a long, dark shadow appeared in the entrance to the chasm. Sisilla waved it away and it departed.

"What a shame," sighed Grandmother. "I would've liked to meet them."

"It probably wouldn't do any good," said Sisilla, smiling. "They can be unintentionally menacing. They scare off intruders. Now we need to continue our journey, but let's eat first. There's a food-machine under the trees over there. We'll take a well-deserved break for a short while."

The Master, Saint Germain, bowed elegantly to Grandmother and showed her to a table with roots in the ground and tree stumps as seating.

In the Great Chasm, Titch had been nervous. It was as though he sniffed out danger, at least for dogs. He sat close to my legs, and I shared the delicious vegetarian food with him. Sisilla, who knew what she was doing, brought us each a different dish. There were spices and salt. The food tasted incredibly good, and a cook on Earth would probably not have been able to produce anything similar. It was served attractively, like a work of art.

I'm looking forward to the next stop, I thought. I was not to be disappointed. Saint Germain vanished while we were eating. He probably didn't need food.

"He was called to another dimension and will return as soon as possible," Sisilla explained. We hurried with our food and stepped back into our trusty vehicle.

Next stop was on the edge of a jungle. I knew this because I had seen jungles many times on television when I lived on Earth. I had always wanted to see a real one. But where were we?

As if she had heard, Sisilla cried, "We are right under an African jungle — the Congo, to be exact. The jungle here is like the one above Earth, but the animals aren't dangerous unless threatened. They have no experience of guns or arrows. The wickedness wreaked on Earth's wild animals is invented, and caused by people.

"Animals eating animals is natural, and part of the food-chain. Here you can walk unharmed if you show no fear. An animal will only threaten if it senses fear. Keep calm, and there is no danger. Let's walk in single file. I'll lead, as I'm used to animals."

She headed off along a narrow path, indicating for us to follow. Edmund stopped suddenly.

"I've had enough of jungles," he remarked, unbuttoning his shirt and pulling out his arm. A bright red scar stretched up the length of his left arm and shoulder, coming dangerously close to his heart.

"I got too close to a tiger," he continued. "I only survived because my friends behind managed to scare it off before it killed me. One of my friends was a skillful doctor, and there was surgical equipment at one of the tourist centers, so he disinfected the tear and sewed it up straight away. Jungles hold no attraction for me."

"You've no need to be scared here," Sisilla said gently. "I guarantee your safety. You can't stay here, as we'll come out elsewhere. The Congo is not much like the jungle here in Agartha. Animals will not attack unprovoked here. Tim will walk with you and then you'll feel safe."

"I can tell you some funny anecdotes," I declared with a smile. "Not about dangerous animals, but about dangerous women." Everyone laughed, and we continued into the jungle.

"Look at this!" said Lex. "Look at these amazing flowers climbing around the trees. They must be some kind of orchid ..."

His calm voice kept us informed about the vegetation in the jungle, as he had been here before. Suddenly, all this luxuriant foliage opened out into a meadow.

"I'm going to ask you to sit on the ground a moment, in a ring," Sisilla instructed us.

"Set aside fear, as we are here to meet animals, and this is a test for your Agarthan residence-permits. We send cowards home. Shut your eyes, and don't open them again before I blow my whistle."

We sat in a ring on the emerald grass among the sweetly scented flowers, the bumblebees, and the butterflies. The grass wasn't as tall as meadow grass, and the flowers were close to the ground. Shutting our eyes made us aware of the heavenly smells wafting around, bringing peace and calm.

Then Sisilla blew the whistle, and we opened our eyes.

Animals were creeping out of the darkness of the trees. There were lions, tigers, elephants, monkeys both big and small, zebras, giraffes, and brown bears. Sisilla was piping caressing melodies, and the animals were as if enchanted.

Edmund was next to me, and Titch wriggled between us, resting his head on his great paws. He watched everything with quivering nostrils, but was quiet as I had instructed.

The row of animals grew. Edmund seized the sleeve of my shirt and held it firmly. He was pale. The animals stopped in front of Sisilla, lowering their heads, and she scratched an ear or a nose. It was a

90

hypnotic moment. I was convinced we were all hypnotized, because this couldn't happen! The animals passed by us singly and in troops, with the pungent smell of wild animal nearly suffocating at times.

Sisilla set aside the whistle and put her hands to her mouth. The peculiar noise she produced had an instant effect on our visitors. They dispersed at once, running for the forest.

"You can rest assured," called our guide, "that nothing would happen if you met these animals alone. They have learned to respect us, as we respect them. This is our last visit for today, and we can carry on tomorrow if you like."

Edmund let go of my shirt with a sigh of relief. He had been overwhelmed by the sight of the animals. He climbed swiftly into the nearby hovercraft.

We followed. Grandmother stooped to pick a flower, but Sisilla stopped her.

"You see," our guide observed gently, "we're not allowed to pick the flowers. Only the growers can take what they need. When you pick a flower, you interfere with the floral group-soul, creating a gap for all eternity. It can't be repaired.

"Flowers which know they will be picked for their smell, spice, or edibility give themselves up bravely, praying for help and forgiveness for the pickers. Everything here is alive, even if it's produced by people. That's one of the secrets of a holistic lifestyle, which is the norm here. It's a system of living imagery."

"How interesting," said my grandmother, smiling. "I won't pick the flowers, I promise. We have to learn the rules if we're going to live here!"

Titch and I climbed into our transport. Lex was already sitting with Grandmother. We took off.

18. The Love Union

The hovercraft landed near our homes. Sisilla went into Grandmother's house. I had kissed Sisilla briefly when we left the meadow after meeting the animals. There had been plenty of trees to conceal us. Grandmother had given us a knowing look and couldn't hide a smile of delight.

I wondered how to go about courting a girl on this side of the planet. I knew Sisilla was the person I wanted to spend the rest of my life with — which looked like it would be a very long time indeed! I wanted children with her, and the opportunity of watching them grow up in this enchanted place. I admit that things had gone very quickly, but time was a different concept here.

We went into Grandmother's house and sat on her comfortable sofa. While Grandmother went into what she called the kitchen to make tea, I took Sisilla's hands and gazed deep into her eyes.

"Will you be my wife?" I asked. I had no idea what weddings were like in this part of the world, but Sisilla laughed, leaned across and kissed my cheek, and answered by singing out "yes" while dancing some graceful steps. I got up and danced with her until Grandmother came with the tea-tray.

"Grandmother Emilie, we're going to get married!" I called out happily. "Sisilla has agreed, and now we have to draw up some plans."

"Let's make it a double wedding!" laughed Grandmother. "I've just accepted Lex to be my husband today!"

Sisilla looked at us in bewilderment. "Double wedding, getting married?" she asked. "I'll be your wife, Tim, and there's a ceremony for that. Is Emilie going to be a wife, too? Lex's? What happens on the surface?"

Grandmother (her eyes shining with tears — she was always

emotional) explained about clothes and a church wedding. She mentioned the vicar and exchanging rings.

Sisilla listened, round-eyed.

"That's not how we do it," she observed quietly. "You'll see how we do it. You are welcome to our Love Union, which will take place tomorrow evening, if that's all right with you, Tim?"

I nodded in the sweet knowledge that I was about to be married to the loveliest girl in the world. I really didn't care about the details. The day ran away just like they do on the surface, even if it was only a feeling of passing time. When Sisilla had gone home, there was a knock on my door. It was Mannul, and I was really glad to see him. I wanted to tell him about my coming "marriage" and ask him what it would be like.

"It's not quite like an Earthly wedding!" he laughed, thumping me on the back. "It's just a Love Union, where both sides decide to continue their lives together. A teacher blesses the union. We don't have divorce, but if one partner should die, then the union is broken. You can only have second thoughts before the union takes place. We don't have vicars, just a symbolic union of body and soul.

"You will both be wearing white. We don't use tiaras and veils; the clothes don't matter as long as they are white. On these occasions, we wear white cloaks to represent the unwritten pages of the future. The couple can be alone or surrounded by relatives and friends. Everyone likes to come, so the bridal couple is rarely alone. In Porthologos, we have special 'bridal suites.' Most people get married there. There will be plenty of onlookers, as 'By Invitation Only' doesn't exist here. The reception afterwards goes on until all hours, and there is food and drink everywhere."

"It sounds exciting," I answered. "What shall we do about rings?"

"You can give each other jewelry. I can help you with that. Women quite often like some kind of token. Otherwise, there is nothing else to distinguish marriage. This evening is your last as a bachelor. You should go home and get a good night's sleep. It's important that you know in your own mind you won't have any regrets."

"There's an entrance, but no exit," I joked. "I can tell you now, I'm 100% sure."

Mannul said, "I'm really here because Arniel needs you in the Town Hall. He wants to discuss your future work. We'll do it later. I'll go and tell him the glad tidings. Now you're really one of us." He thumped me on the back.

"Sisilla was born here and doesn't know much about the world outside. Our people are one entity, under the flag of Unity. The circle represents unity, and is a much-used symbol. I'll return tomorrow when I've found some circle jewelry for you and your bride."

"Emilie needs to know this, too!" I called. "She's going to marry Lex, preferably at the same time as us. Will that be alright?"

"That will be completely wonderful," Mannul replied. "But they need to know the traditions. I can help them, because Lex won't know everything yet."

I sighed with relief as my fair friend shut the door behind him. It was great he was around to help. I needed to sleep a few hours before dawn, which arrives invisibly here. In the end, I slept like a baby, and didn't wake up until a panting Titch placed his paws on my stomach and licked me in the face. A rude awakening!

Behind him was Mannul, holding something white. It turned out to be my wedding clothes. The clothes didn't include tails or a dinner jacket. They were soft trousers and a baggy jacket, with an ankle-length cloak. This last had richly-decorated shoulder ornaments attached.

"There we go!" Mannul cocked his head to one side and surveyed me with a critical eye. Then he put a sparkling band of white around Titch's black neck, which didn't seem to bother my dog in the least. He yawned, and stared amiably at Mannul, who was holding exquisitely beautiful jewels in his hands. It was a necklace with a pendant that glittered with diamonds. Diamonds were commonplace here and beautiful. The pendant was heart-shaped, with a ruby in the center, an artwork by a goldsmith.

"Love Unions take place in the mornings here," Mannul continued, "as early as possible. Your grandmother and her husband-to-be are ready, and your bride is waiting impatiently in the bridal suite."

I followed Mannul rapidly outside to the waiting hovercraft. We landed at an entrance to Porthologos, and Mannul led us upstairs and downstairs, along winding corridors, and through temple halls and lovely inside gardens. Soft music accompanied us everywhere. We stopped at the gate to one of the gardens. It was decorated with images of butterflies and roses. We were approaching a raised area swathed in flowers.

Sisilla was there, radiating such beauty that my stomach tied itself in knots and I gasped for breath. Like me, she was in white, but her white, ankle-length dress glinted like moonbeams and her amazing hairstyle was crowned with diamonds. My gift glittered on her breast, and she was holding a chain with a similar heart on it. She put this around my neck and took my hand. At our side were Grandmother and her bridegroom, both in white. I nearly didn't recognize my grandmother. She was so attractive with her long, white hair, rosy cheeks, and tears of happiness brimming in her cornflower eyes. Lex was handsome, more Indian-like than ever, with his clear-cut profile and tanned complexion.

Master Arniel appeared suddenly from the shadows. He smiled at the four of us. Then he came to each of us and placed his hands on our brows. Afterwards, he beckoned Sisilla and me to the pillared podium.

"Hug your wife!" he commanded, and we stood close, embracing, while wonderful music played and time stood still. It was as though an incredible force closed around us and everything else vanished. We were one, wholly united, as if we lived in each other and were each other. It was a magical moment, and lasted for ages. I couldn't say how long; it felt like an eternity, but was probably only a few minutes in our time.

The music ended and Arniel gestured for us to leave the podium. Grandmother and Lex rose to get up. In the garden were four flowery chairs where we sat and surveyed the scene we had just experienced. We were still holding hands and exchanging looks of love. Grandmother and Lex joined us for about half an hour, I think, with Arniel close by.

"Now you are joined in matrimony, as you say on the surface," declared Arniel. "We don't consider words necessary for this ceremony.

Now you may do as you please. You may go home, as I guarantee there'll be a crowd outside waiting to congratulate you … here they are now!"

He hardly had time to complete his sentence before the garden filled with people and elementals who I glimpsed briefly as a glow. Arniel saw my confusion and laid a hand on my shoulder.

"Some of Sisilla's relatives and friends are five-dimensional," he told me. "They may be indistinct, but are devoted for all that."

We were fairly overwhelmed by wedding guests, if I can call them that. They were all gate-crashers! The only person invited was Edmund, who came with Wendy and Pierre. A dance started up, and delightful singing, which whirled faster and faster, submerging our thoughts and senses. The place pulsed with rhythm, tempestuous dance, and joyful, stirring music. I was glad when Saint Germain appeared from nowhere and hugged us.

"We'll meet again soon," he said. "I'm releasing Sisilla from guide duties tomorrow, as she's a newly-wed. I'll take over."

Someone must've been holding Titch during the wedding ceremony, because now he pushed through the crush of bodies and came to my side, his head held high with intense vigilance. The diamond collar glittered on his black neck, and people withdrew to a safe distance.

"I want to go home," I whispered to my new wife. She nodded, eyes sparkling. She took my hand and Titch's collar, and hey presto, everything vanished. We were at home, and Titch retired to bed.

19. Back to Normality and Tourists in Agartha

The day dawned sunny and summery, with birdsong and the scent of flowers, warm ground, and trees. My wife and I were sitting in the arbor when Mannul turned up.

"The holiday is over!" he cried out. "It's time to get back to work!"

We sighed, and climbed into the waiting hovercraft.

"There are newcomers who need to know about this part of the planet." Mannul explained. "We need Sisilla to give a short introduction on Telos, as they won't get further than that. They came through Mount Shasta, but they don't really believe they're awake yet. They think they're dreaming. They'll have to wake up sometime!"

The "tourists" were waiting in the meadow near the entrance to Porthologos. Grandmother, Lex, and Titch were among them, so I joined them because I still wanted to know more about Agartha, which I was now attached to for eternity.

People were sitting on the grass, excited and expectant.

Mannul was among them, smiling and talking, probably in an attempt to calm them down, as they didn't know where they were. I thought about coming here "by accident" (to my mind) and imagined they had all had a similar experience.

There were about twenty adults, but no children other than Wendy and Pierre. Sisilla was utterly charming. It was as though my wife projected a supernatural beam into each of us.

"Welcome!" she called. "If you are wondering where in the world you are, I'm about to inform you. This town is Telos, and it is in the subterranean part of the Earth, the existence of which you have not yet acknowledged. You only recognize seven continents: Africa, Asia, Europe, North America, South America, Oceania, and Antarctica.

"According to you, this continent inside the Earth does not exist. But I'm telling you it does, even physically for the three-dimensional people here. Telos is the largest town, apart from the capital, which is called Shamballa. None of our towns here are like your noisy cities, where evil lurks around every corner. This is the kingdom of eternal Peace which you pine for with nostalgia on the surface.

"Yes, nostalgia! Originally, we Agarthans are from the surface, just like you. There are books about us, but they are not best-sellers. You imagine a Hollow Earth country to be gray and dangerous. But it's not like that, as you can see. As far as technology is concerned, we are light-years ahead of you surface-dwellers! We hope to share our knowledge with you in the future. That future is closer than you think.

"The network of Agartha embraces 120 underground towns. The inhabitants of these towns are descended from the advanced civilizations of Atlantis and Lemuria.

"I'm sure you are wondering, how can we have our own sun here providing good weather and verdant foliage? The Earth's crust is approximately 800 miles (1 300 km) thick. The planet isn't solid, so the center of gravity isn't in the center of the Earth, but in the Earth's crust, about 400 miles (650 km) underground. The source of the Earth's magnetism has long been a mystery. The inner sun in the center of the Earth is the mysterious source of Earth's magnetism. It shines upon us here.

"There was an inventor at the end of the 19th century called Nikola Tesla. At that time, there were many entrances into the Earth's hollow interior. Tesla discovered that electricity could be harnessed in unlimited quantities to power all machinery, without the need for coal, oil, gas, or any other environmental pollutant. He placed this technology in the public domain, and people began to abuse entry to the Earth's interior, so that we had to seal off many portals, and they remain sealed. Tesla himself vanished, and actually he is here, but less physical than you these days.

"Many million Catharians live here in the Hollow Earth. Catharians also live on Jupiter. I'm telling you this because the Catharians are a strange people. They are incredibly tall, even in their stocking feet! More than 36,000 people from the surface live here now. In the last 200 years, about 50 people have arrived from the surface, but in the last 20 years, 8 people have moved here permanently. Some of the newcomers are with us now, and other visitors are arriving, like you today.

"We have an enormous library called Porthologos. It contains documents from the entire universe. It is under the Aegean Sea (between Greece and Turkey), but nowadays no longer has a direct link with the surface. We call it a library, although it doesn't contain many books! We have historical stories related dramatically. It's like theater, but more so. There is much more in Porthologos which we will show you, in part at least.

"Within Agartha, no passports or papers are needed. We have airports inside the Earth, which lead to openings, concealed from your eyes, at the North and South Poles. We travel in an environmentally-friendly way, using existing highways, and the universal laws of energy. Our technology is so much in advance of yours that we can't get lost or have an accident. You may have invented the wheel, but you haven't gotten much further.

"All our energy is free. You could use this same energy, and we are planning to teach you how it works. You have abused technology, using it to build weapons. These are destructive, not only for the intended target, but also for the animal kingdom and elementals."

Emilie put up her hand and called out, "Sisilla, please tell us more about living here! We need to know, now that we've come to live in Telos."

Sisilla continued, "First and foremost, we don't like destroying the ground which you surface-dwellers walk on. We want grass and flowers to grow without being trampled on. That's why we have learned to hover, which you will also learn if you stay here. Hovercrafts do it, and we do too. This lawn is made especially for heavy surface-dwellers like you, but there aren't many places like this. We are taller than you in comparison, but lighter, because of the food we eat.

"Emilie wanted to know about our home life. Of course we have one! We build the round, roofless houses you've already seen. A round room never gets dusty, as there are no corners. Energy moves freely in a circular room. When a speck of dust flies into a room, it is removed on a wave of energy. It has the same effect as a vacuum cleaner, without the bag. This is practical, to say the least.

"We are incredibly rich, because we have precious stones and metals in abundance. Our homes are luminous. Externally, there is privacy. Inside, we have a 360-degree view. On the surface, you are locked in dark rooms, while we can see not only outside our homes, but right up to the stars. Our field of vision is unimpeded. Apart from our houses, there are no shopping centers, no blocks of flats, no motorways."

"What do you do about food?" someone called. "Are you all vegetarians?" Sisilla grinned.

"You bet!" she replied. "No animals are killed here for food. We eat fruit, vegetables, seeds, and grains. There is no life force in what we call dead food, by which we mean meat, fowl, and fish. There are distribution centers where we can obtain food for each day. Some of us get food from the universal Source, which only requires concentration.

"A working day lasts four hours, which gives us time to spare and time to take our health and diet into consideration. We live harmoniously, without hurry or stress. Nothing is wasted; we have advanced methods of recycling. We eat only locally-produced food, and don't add chemicals to it. A vegetarian diet has slowed and finally stopped the aging process, and we have achieved what you call immortality. We have full control of our aging and can lengthen our lives as we wish."

"What a lovely life!" sighed Grandmother, and many burst out laughing. They probably couldn't believe it, and would be unable to follow this regime.

"What about clothes?" called a very elegant lady. Sisilla laughed and spread out the skirt of her long dress, which was fastened with a sparkling belt.

"How about this?" she asked. "Our fashion may be considered uncomfortable and boring by Earthlings. Of course, we have a choice of materials and tailors, but not in the same way as you. The latest Paris fashion doesn't enter into it! We like soft, wearable clothes in beautiful colors.

"We use capes outdoors if necessary. We know you wear jeans, shirts, and jumpers, but we only wear those if we are visiting the surface. I think we are clothes-conscious and wear imaginative clothing, but maybe you don't agree?"

The elegant lady giggled, but didn't reply. She looked horrified when Sisilla added, "My dear, we produce things by thought in this part of the world. We create by thinking." She was quiet, and shut her eyes a moment. With a wave of her hand, she produced a wonderful bouquet of flowers. Everyone screamed and probably thought it was sorcery.

I didn't like the atmosphere at this juncture. I went and put my arm around my wife's shoulder. Then I looked at the elegant lady, who seemed to have turned to stone, an ugly look on her face.

"Ladies and gentlemen!" I announced. "You are here to learn about this part of the planet. My wife has told you a great deal. She is no enchantress. Anyone can learn direct creation by the power of thought, but you need quiet and patience. It doesn't involve magic, sorcery, or witchcraft. It involves knowledge. Knowledge on the surface hasn't developed to the extent which we Agarthans take for granted. Here everyone is a magician, to use layman's terms.

"I suggest that those who can't accept our culture leave our inner Earth and return to the rat-race on the surface. You ought not enter Porthologos, because it presents even greater challenges."

I took the bouquet which Sisilla was still holding, and threw it out into the audience. There was a moment of silence, and then applause. But the elegant lady stood up without glancing in our direction, and vanished into a waiting hovercraft. Most of the rest of us entered the amazing, shimmering library known as Porthologos. A few of the visitors remained outside, discussing what they had just heard. They simply didn't dare enter. No-one on the surface would ever believe the stories they could tell, so maybe they should just return and keep quiet about the mysterious land they had visited.

We wandered around the lovely, immense building, watching holographic images of the past and future. It is difficult to describe Porthologos. It really has to be experienced firsthand. It's a weird mixture of the physical, the psychic, facts, and entertainment. For people on the surface, the past is available in fairly reliable books, but the future is yet unwritten. Here, the past and the future are accessible to everyone. You can play with time as you choose, or go beyond time. In this context, things may seem scary and unfathomable, but when you are here, it becomes completely natural.

We were resting, catching our breath in one of the common rooms. Edmund, sitting beside me and my wife, asked, "There's something we've avoided talking about, and that's illness. Is there a hospital here, and doctors? How does the health system work? Do you not get ill?"

"Oh yes, there is illness," replied Sisilla, "but not much. We break arms and legs, and have problems with internal organs. We're just human, you know. But we have healers to help with illness and accidents. If you lose a limb, you can get a new one. We exchange worn-out body organs for new ones. There are as many skillful healers as there are problems. You can't lose or maim a limb in your etheric blueprint, so from this eternal blueprint we can restore any lost or maimed physical body parts."

"What about mental health if you're in need of a shrink?" asked a young man with fine, dark hair, which he shook continuously. I laughed.

"We're all shrinks," I pointed out. "We have many wise men and women who help when necessary. They have endless patience, and the ability to guide us through problems." I remembered how dreadful I had felt after the shipwreck, and what a short time it took to get back to normal. I mostly had my friend Mannul to thank for that.

"There aren't any televisions, telephones, or radios," a very young man called out. "How do you communicate with each other?"

Sisilla's laughter rang out. "We use our brains and thoughts!" she answered. "We accomplish all we need with the power of thought. You haven't really figured out how it works up there on the surface, Valencio, my dear!"

The young man looked harassed. "How do you know my name?" he snapped. "In Italy, where I come from, we Catholics don't allow any mumbo-jumbo. The Pope, my father, wants us to keep to the Holy Scripture."

"The Pope is your father?" I asked, flummoxed. "Do you mention that in Italy? You must've been a sin of his youth, surely?"

"I don't think so," Valencio replied calmly. "That's why I'm traveling. I found out about Agartha from one of the high priests, Cardinal Reimfort. He's French, and has always been kind to me. I know what goes on behind the scenes at the Vatican. That's why they're looking for me now: I'm a wanted man. I've always longed to be anywhere apart from where I grew up. I think I'd like to stay here. What religion do you believe in — you do have a religion?"

"Tourists are allowed to stay for two days," I commented.

I relented when I saw the look of disappointment on the boy's face. "I can ask, if you really want to stay longer. You'll have to ask my wife about religion."

Sisilla gestured to the boy to sit, and he sat down at her feet.

"I was brought up in a monastery," he said. "We were treated cruelly and beaten with a stick! When I finished school, I was forced to live at the Vatican as a kind of novice.

"My relationship to the Pope was completely hushed up. My father pretended not to recognize me, even though sometimes I had to serve him. He never looked me in the eye. The only friend I had was Cardinal Reimfort, and he taught me much more than Greek and Latin. Otherwise I was regarded as a thug, although I tried to be as observant as possible.

"My attentiveness meant that I noticed much that was taboo. I can tell you more of this later. Reimfort told me the Earth was hollow and that you could get here by sea, or via Mount Shasta. I ran away. I stole some money that was lying around and took a plane to South America. It was easy. Now I'm wanted for stealing, although I consider the money mine by right, as I was never given a penny, while the old men in the Vatican drank and ate well and were sensuous in the bargain."

He paused for breath, and I interrupted.

"Valencio," I said. "Thank you for being so honest. You should really be locked up, but we don't do that here. I'll speak to the powers that be and see what they say. Until then, you can live with Edmund, who has two scamps you can help look after."

Edmund had listened to this confession in its entirety and couldn't help laughing. "The Vatican, oh my goodness, the Vatican!" he chuckled, slapping his thighs. "He can certainly live with us, there's plenty of room. He can't steal money here, but maybe he should send some precious stones to His Holiness the Pope, when he has earned some, with a politely respectful, affectionate letter!"

Valencio looked confused, but then giggled too.

I tried to look strict, but it's not one of my strong points. "How old are you?" I asked the boy.

"Nineteen, soon twenty," was the reply. "Please don't return me to the surface! The Vatican has spies everywhere, and I'll be taken into custody at Mount Shasta. Cardinal Reimfort will guess where I am, although he won't tell. He's the only one of them who has a decent heart."

"Politics and religion!" exclaimed my new "grandfather" Lex. "My dear Sisilla, what are your views on these important subjects?"

My wife's smile froze on her face. It was obvious that these subjects were not dear to her heart. "Actually Lex, my dear, we don't really get involved," she replied. "Throughout Agartha, we have only one religion: our belief in the eternal Source, the dwelling place of Love. There aren't any dissenters or free-thinkers. We are all One in this Love. We call our belief the Faith of Light. Everything is one in Love."

"Yes, but who is in control here? Somebody or some group must govern the country." It was Edmund's turn to ask, and Valencio's face reflected wonder and anxiety.

"Of course," I replied. "We are governed by a Council of twelve Masters. Twelve is the magic number for endings. That's why Mayan culture has predicted changes to the Earth in 2012."

"I know, but you aren't allowed to mention that in the Vatican!" retorted Valencio. "I have my own religion in my mind. My father

106

is in heaven, as he doesn't acknowledge my existence on Earth, Pope that he is."

I realized the sense of bitterness this young man felt towards his father and his tough upbringing. "Is your mother alive?" I asked.

"No," Valencio replied, and I could see he was fighting back tears. "A man isn't allowed to cry" was still part of his world-view, formed by rigid monks in secret, where a strict God judged the human heart.

"My mother died a few months after my birth," the dark-haired boy continued. "I don't think she died of natural causes. They said she died of complications after giving birth, in an effort to blame me. Cardinal Reimfort helped relieve my conscience.

"My mother was the daughter of a rich, respected nobleman who owned large estates in south-east Italy, near the Pope's childhood home. She was disowned and cast out by her parents, who looked upon me as a bastard with no right to live. I probably would've been killed if Cardinal Reimfort hadn't argued my case, and I was taken in by thick-skinned monks instead. That's my life-history. I would like to stay here. The monks taught me well: astronomy, geology, advanced mathematics, French, English, and Latin, of course. Might I be of some use?"

"We'll see what we can do," answered Sisilla gently, giving the boy a lovely smile. "Any more questions before we split up?"

"Are there taxes here, or don't you use money at all? How do you pay for things when you buy food, clothes, or houses? Or are you just allocated these things? Doesn't anybody earn a wage?" My inquisitive grandmother was on the case again.

"Not in the same way as on the surface, Grandmother," I replied. "We exchange goods, and there are centers for goods everywhere. We take only what we need, and return things when we have finished using them. We swap with each other.

"We make things ourselves. The four-hour working day is very intense, and if we can't organize something, there is always someone else to help with planning or whatever. We don't buy, we share!"

"What about law and order, then? Are there police, lawyers, and judiciary?" These questions came from Lex.

"We have laws, yes," I answered. "The legal system is ancient. There has been democracy here since the beginning of time. Agartha's network is responsible for our safety underground. Cases that arise and need solutions are considered individually and judged in God's Light and the holy code of Justice. Our long lives provide experience and wisdom. There aren't many difficult cases here. Many of the ancients here lived on the surface originally, and know how to differentiate between good and bad."

"I think we should sleep on this until a new day brings us new energy!" Edmund called out, with two slumbering children at his side. Titch gave a short bark and raised his enormous weight, looking enquiringly at me and Sisilla. Valencio went with Edmund and the children. A small fleet of hovercraft waited patiently in the rose-colored light which came at the end of the bright golden day, bringing promise of the heavenly cradle of sleep.

20. The Purpose of Pets

We were awakened by Titch's indiscreet scratching and panting. It was time for the next stage in discovering the culture of this remarkable land. I suddenly thought of something at breakfast, and I was devastated.

"Sisilla! What about your parents?" I asked suddenly, seizing her hands, which had been busy crumbling her bread.

"What about them?" she asked, putting some bread into her mouth.

"I've always presumed they were dead," I said. "You've never talked about them. We should've invited them to our Love Union if they're alive. Do you have any siblings?"

"We've actually forgotten to talk about these things," replied my wife. "My parents live in the fifth dimension, a long way away. They know of our union and gave their approval. So far, you can only see three dimensions, so you wouldn't have noticed if they had come. I have a sister and a brother. They are also five-dimensional, but you can meet them all when you're ready. I crossed the boundary when I lived in Telos for a while. It's not the first time I've been three-dimensional, as I love Earthlings and want to help educate them. Now I'm married to one, although you will also become five-dimensional."

"Now I really don't understand," I sighed. "If you were five-dimensional, I wouldn't be able to see you. I know there are both kinds in Telos ..."

"And you know that five-dimensional beings have the capacity to transform themselves when they want," interrupted my wife.

"But ... if we have children," I stammered. "What would happen to them? Would they be a mixture?"

Sisilla's peal of laughter removed my anxiety.

"You've got a lot to learn," she hooted. "The things you don't understand yet …" She got up from the table and danced into the garden with me following. Mannul was there.

"I was just about to visit you turtle doves!" he said, smiling. "Arniel wants to see you, remember, Tim?"

I was a bit embarrassed that I'd forgotten. Mannul apologized to Sisilla for leaving her alone on this beautiful morning, and then I was off in his hovercraft, wondering if I would learn anything exciting, like how to become five-dimensional.

"Not yet," Mannul said, obviously reading my thoughts. "It's not far off, but you have some work to put in first."

"That stuff about dimensions —" I started to say.

"— is very complicated." My friend finished the sentence.

"Here we are." I jumped down. Titch had volunteered to stay with Sisilla. He loved her and the garden, and she liked playing with him.

Like many other buildings, the one before us now was inlaid with jewels. The interior glittered with gold and other precious metals in ingenious patterns. Arniel was sitting in a comfortable armchair, gesturing for us to sit down.

"Now you're a serious member of Agarthan society, Tim!" He smiled. "You have married the daughter of original inhabitants. This makes us happy, and we offer our congratulations. But there is a genetic disparity, in that Sisilla has more genes than you. Now you're married to a native, we'll have to transfer some more to you. At the same time, we want you as our special envoy to interact with the surface. It's possible to do both. We need people like you on the surface. Things may be different now you have a family, which may well grow. You need to learn more telepathy and many other 'magic tricks,' as you like to call them. We have put this off until you were really one of us. Mannul will come for you every day, and lessons will take place in a variety of locations, starting tomorrow. That is my message."

I was pleased with this, and so was Sisilla.

It was a four-way celebration, as Grandmother and Lex threw an Earth-style party for us. Even my "little" Titch was invited. He always knew something special was going on when he wore his wide red collar with gold studs and a rosette. So far, we hadn't met any pet dogs. I wondered why, and decided to find out more about pets in this world.

There's no real difference between morning and evening in Agartha. The sun always shines. We decide ourselves how we want to divide up the day, and we sleep when we need to. Many people keep regular hours, just as on Earth. As we trotted over to Grandmother and Lex's, we decided it was evening. Actually, we hovered across, our feet carefully above the ground. We'd learned how to do this, and it's not as weird as it sounds. In this way, we didn't destroy any plants.

My grandmother had set out a Swedish smorgasbord, as far as possible. Swedes love their smorgasbord and like to indulge, even abroad. Grandmother still had some treats she had brought with her, like crispbread, ginger thins, and dried meat. All we needed was schnapps and beer, but instead we had wine from Telos.

Mannul was invited too, and seemed somewhat confused to see the groaning table. He kept to the vegetables from Telos. Titch was given a meaty bone and danced around in delight.

"I'm going to take this opportunity to ask a question," I said, as we were sitting outside among trailing flowers and leaves. Grapes grew like a roof over us, and the scents from the warm ground were almost overwhelming. "Do people keep dogs here, or are they considered unclean, like in Oriental countries on the surface?"

"Don't worry." Mannul smiled. "There are all kinds of pets here. But we don't walk them like you do. We always have a purpose if we're walking, and it may be difficult to take a pet along. We use cats and dogs therapeutically when necessary. Don't you up there," he lifted his hand to point at the roof of grapes, "realize the healing properties of cats, dogs, and horses? There aren't any healers here who don't use them in their treatment. It's important to keep the animals clean and cultivate their intelligence properly. They're not allowed to run around willy-nilly. Does that answer your question?"

I stroked Titch as he sniffed my arm, which obviously smelled interesting. "What a shame he hasn't learned that," I commented.

Mannul's smile widened. "Titch is going to learn all about it. He's coming on our field-trip tomorrow. He'll be learning at the same time as you!"

That sounded great, if mysterious. I was being educated with my dog. That was a slightly mad thought.

21. Lessons Begin

So what happened to Valencio? He came to Grandmother's party. We had quite a good chat about his escape, his misgivings, hopes, and great sadness that his father didn't care for him. He regarded himself as an orphan and wanted to stay with us. Mannul promised to ask the Galactic Council if they could give him a home in Agartha, or another planet. In the meantime, he lived with Edmund and the children, where he was very popular.

It seemed that Sisilla knew more about the lessons Mannul would provide than I had supposed. When I expressed concern at leaving her so soon after our Love Union, she consoled me that it wouldn't be for long. Many lessons could take place at home, and she would be there too. Apart from that, she had her own daily chores and I had to remember that no-one worked longer than four hours each day in Agartha. After that, your time was your own. It was strange how all tasks seemed to fit into the allotted time. This could be achieved on Earth, too, if people were more disciplined.

Mannul arrived punctually the next morning. I had come to rely upon this tall, slim man with his long, blond hair and friendly demeanor. I felt totally secure with him.

Titch did too, and showed his enthusiasm as we got into the hovercraft. He wagged his tail constantly and tried to push between Mannul and me — not easy in such a small space.

The hovercraft stopped in the countryside outside Telos. As I stepped out, I could see a farmer working in a wheat-field. We walked over to him. He was carrying a seed-bin on his shoulders and sowing the seed by hand. I was surprised, as I knew how easy this would be with a tractor, on the surface.

Suddenly, a host of Nature Spirits appeared, elementals as tall as humans, yet so fragile they were hardly visible at first.

"We work with Nature Spirits here," remarked the farmer, shaking my hand firmly. "They check that the seeds are in the right position to maintain vitality. That's the secret of all the seed here: Its vitality remains in all you eat. Devas yearn to return to the surface to help."

"Close your eyes, Tim!" Mannul ordered.

I closed them. When I was allowed to open them again, we were in the middle of a field of golden wheat, glowing with ripeness. The farmer at our side laughed and called, "This is what you get if you don't spray it with rubbish, but allow the crop to grow as it will."

I could see it was excellent grain, even if there was an occasional cornflower, poppy, or daisy adding an undeniable charm to the mass of gold.

"You have to remember," Mannul observed, as we walked with the farmer, "that on the surface you ship food from all over. Food imported from other lands cannot increase your vitality, as it doesn't receive the right local encouragements. It introduces something alien into your body, which often strikes a discordant note with your inherited frequency. In fact, you could say that you are consuming the thoughts and feelings of unfamiliar people, and these are then transferred to you. This affects your internal organs, unbeknownst to you. Ingesting thoughts from other countries may increase fears and phobias previously dormant. You're left wondering where those thoughts and ideas came from."

"Is that true?" I yelled in horror, feeling like a cannibal. "I just want to be myself!"

"You are yourself; don't panic!" Mannul laughed, thumping me on the back. "But surface-dwellers will have to return to Nature. Things aren't looking good for them."

While we were talking, Titch had been sniffing around and cocking his leg here and there. When he sat down to do his business, I tried to stop him, but the farmer restrained me.

"The best manure we have comes from animals," he said.

"We bring manure from towns and houses to use on arable land. Human excrement is pulverized in situ, and mixed with dung to a sandy, non-smelly powder. The best growth is the result of natural manure, not artificial like they use up there." He pointed skywards. It was strange to think of artificially-fertilized fields hanging just over our heads. Of course, it was a good way off.

We were in the hovercraft again.

"That was a great lesson," I beamed. "I'm glad there are farmers here, and that they reap a good harvest without too much effort."

"It's not a matter of effort," Mannul answered. "We are willing, and we work hard. It owes a lot to the goodwill of Mother Earth, as we don't add artificial fertilizer. Now we are going to have a lesson on beliefs."

22. The Temple of Belief and a Meeting with Melchizedek

"We talked about religion yesterday when your grandmother mentioned it," Mannul remarked, as the hovercraft stopped in a circular garden with a small building in the center. We alighted and Titch became interested in sniffing the huge number of bushes. The small, round building was like all other buildings, exquisitely beautiful and decorated with precious stones in an ornamental pattern.

"This is a temple," Mannul told me. "We don't have churches and priests of various beliefs as on the surface, but we do have small temples where a priest and priestess act as a link to the Godhead. There's only one divine power. We are aware of that here, and if we aren't, we soon discover it. Come with me!"

I trotted after my friend with the long, fair hair, into the round building. A wide beam of light fell from the open roof — I couldn't understand where it came from.

I knelt down like Mannul — it felt right. I felt encircled by the Light, overwhelmed by gentle warmth as all tensions and unwelcome thoughts dissolved and vanished. I was the light and the light was me. It wasn't just a lovely thought, it was the Truth. The existence was literally an existence made of light.

I don't know if I was asleep or having a vision. I had knelt in respect for the light, and had closed my eyes. When I opened them, I was sitting on a soft sofa in front of the wide light beam. A voice came from it and I shivered with goose pimples. It was so holy ... so sacred.

"Humans, Human Children! A wonderful existence was created for you on beautiful, tranquil Earth, as part of a great family. You worked together, ate and drank together, slept together, and life was all enjoyment, beauty, and Love. Above all, Love!

"This lasted for a relatively short time. When darkness came forth and nearly extinguished the light, you were blinded by acceptance. You accepted a life of Love and you accepted, without question, the encroaching darkness.

"You believed things were as they should be. This became a new life-style and encouraged alien influences and dark deeds. The darkness seeped into your minds in many ways, often disguised as light. You invented religions, which was unnecessary, as there is only one God: one God-consciousness.

"You gave this God as many guises as grains of sand on a beach.

"You believed you had chosen or inherited a religion full of mysticism, stimulating your brains. You were unquestioning.

"You were caught in your own trap and were inspired to struggle, to be envious and jealous. Golden Mammon was the root of all inspiration."

"All this is going to change, isn't it?" I objected. "The new belief for the new age will be in one leader: the God within us who leads to the Highest Source."

"Well answered, Timothy! You may proceed!" The voice was happy and friendly, and Mannul patted me gently on the shoulder.

"You're one of us officially now, Tim," he whispered. "You have met one of the Holy Ones."

"Do you have those here too?" I wondered in surprise. "I didn't think you had Holy Ones as we do on Earth."

"We don't." Mannul sounded slightly offended. "This is a help center. Our temples welcome all those in need of help and support. Our priests and priestesses are wise, highly-developed beings who can cure mental disorder and other problems. I wanted you to know that there are centers like these across our world. You ought to have them too."

"I am no longer an Earthling," I interrupted him. "But these places would definitely be useful on the surface. It's nice to know there are temples like these."

"Everyone comes here," Mannul replied. "There are parties, singing, dancing, and various meetings. The temples have all kinds of uses, apart from protection and sanctuary for those who most need it. And it doesn't cost a thing!" This last sentence was accompanied by a peal of laughter.

The hovercraft was outside, as was Titch, progressing slowly and calmly from shrub to shrub, his tail held high. He nearly bowled us over with happiness when we eventually emerged from the strange house. The journey continued.

We alighted at the entrance to a magnificent, circular amphitheater with stairs descending to an oval stage. I thought it was the Coliseum at Rome. On the stage was a large oval table. Twelve men and women were seated around it. I realized it was the Council of Twelve in Telos.

"Let's go and meet them!" suggested Mannul eagerly.

"We don't want to disturb them!" I didn't want to end up in an investigation which was none of my business.

"We won't! Come on, Tim and Titch!" He hurried down the circular flight of stairs and I followed doubtfully. Titch was busy trying to smell everything.

As we arrived, a man rose and embraced Mannul and then me. It was Saint Germain. Titch was patted too. "Welcome! Sit by me, Tim, and learn a little about our society and the problems which arise here."

I looked around the table. Saint Germain explained who the people were and the offices they held. There were six men and six women.

"An equal distribution," I remarked. "That doesn't happen on Earth."

"There are no differences in the rights of men and women here," Saint Germain replied. "The Council discusses and makes decisions about possible crimes, which are rare, arguments between neighbors, also rare, food problems, and new nourishment ideas. And, of course, our eternal discussion: the surface of the Earth and how we can save it. Great things are happening up there," he pointed to the sky, "and there will soon be changes for the Earthlings. They have manhandled our wounded planet so harshly that the damage is obvious even here. We can't allow that. But who can control the wind?"

"No-one can. So something must be done before things decline

seriously for us because of the negligence and ignorance of Earthlings."
A woman was speaking. She looked middle-aged, tall, dark-haired, and
beautiful. Her name was Lady Nada.

"I lived on the Earth a long time ago," she continued. "At that time,
singing was a great experience, and there were many genres for various
voices. Now singing seems to be an incessant out-of-tune screech. There
are no melodies.

"Very few singers have any training like we had. The music now
played on Earth is damaging the planet. It damages the people who
listen and the energy of the tones. Music can be exalting, but it is
destructive when there is no harmony. I want to help with those
changes. The music of the spheres shall be restored to Mother Earth."

There was approval of this and some clapping.

"The imminent changes will include even your work, my dear Lady
Nada," remarked a man's voice. "I'm Melchizedek, king of kings, and
I'm going to introduce some sense to these Earthlings. Good manners
and positive thinking!"

The man was incredibly impressive. He was tall and strong, yet lithe.
He had long, wavy dark hair and his eyes were bright and captivating.
They were brown with golden flecks. He had a clear and handsome
profile, emanating strength and Love. I thought there was something
Indian in his appearance. His smile was incredibly bright and friendly.
When he smiled, you smiled too, and enjoyed smiling in his company.

"At the moment, most of our meetings in Agartha are about helping
our Earth neighbors," Saint Germain resumed. "This boy," he was
indicating me, "will help us. He hasn't been here long, and has just
married our Sisilla." Everyone cheered, and I could feel myself blushing.

Mannul saved the day. "We're on a field-trip," he called. "Please
may we return for further information at a later date?"

We bowed low and respectfully to the distinguished assembly, and
Mannul and I retreated. Titch didn't. He circled the whole table, sniffing
at each person, being patted, and licking in return. When he came back
to us he stood up on his hind legs, a gesture which denoted approval.
He was entitled to the ensuing applause.

The loyal (or previously programmed) hovercraft was waiting for us. I felt exhausted after the Council meeting and Mannul suggested that we should continue the next day. Thus I hurried home to my waiting wife.

23. Visiting the In-Laws

"I'm coming with you today!" declared Sisilla. She was standing at the foot of the bed, and the morning light swathed her like a glittering, shimmering aura. "We're going to the Bridge of Mists, the boundary between Telos and its surroundings and the enormous country of the fifth dimension. You've been to Shamballa."

"Well, very briefly indeed," I replied. "I'd like to see more of it!"

"You will, darling. My parents live there, and we are going to visit."

At long last, I thought. I hope they'll like me.

"What if they don't like me?"

"Then they'll dissolve our Love Union sensitively. But it won't happen. We love each other, and that's the most important thing for them. Love is paramount from the fifth dimension upwards. Agartha IS Love! Hurry up and get changed, I've ordered a hovercraft. Titch is coming with us."

Titch wolfed down his breakfast of vegetarian dog food, which he had come to enjoy. I don't think he'd forgotten the meat he used to eat, but Titch is probably the only Great Dane alive who lives on vegetables and appreciates them. I hadn't seen many dogs of his size here, but then again, I hadn't seen many animals here at all. I dressed in a white shirt and white trousers, and put a diamond-studded white collar on Titch.

Sisilla was in a pink creation with a matching wide-brimmed hat. She looked amazing. We entered the hovercraft, which immediately gained altitude.

My grandmother used to sing this Swedish marching song:

> "In summer's sunny glow,
> Through woods and fields we go,
> Worries we do not know,
> Singing all the way, hurray, hurray …"

I whistled it now as the ground disappeared and we ascended to a good height. I'm actually pretty good at whistling.

My wife gave me an amused look. "That was a lovely tune," she smiled and said.

"I can play more old Swedish songs on the piano," I replied, "if we can get hold of one."

"I know which instrument you mean," returned Sisilla. "We can probably create one if you like."

I hadn't thought of that, but this was obviously the land of opportunities. I decided to create a grand piano at home as soon as possible. Creative forces were unrestrained here in Agartha, as long as they were positive. This was something I'd learned right from my first time here, otherwise I wouldn't have had a bed to sleep in. Sisilla had created a lovely home for us. It was pretty, cosy, and practical.

The hovercraft headed downwards and landed in a place so misty that you could hardly see your hand in front of your face. Titch walked close to me; he didn't like being out of sight. Sisilla waved both hands and the fog dissipated slightly so that we could make out the bridge we were standing on, with its tall, carved railings reaching up and forming an archway above us. Under the bridge ran clear rapids, culminating in a small waterfall a little further downstream. I could just make out the contours of a forest on either side.

"We are on the bridge which separates the third and fifth dimensions," she announced.

"You mean the third and fourth dimensions?" I suggested.

"No, I mean the third and the fifth. The fourth doesn't exist here," she replied. It sounded strange to me, but I let it go for now. I didn't realize how soon I would find out more.

The Bridge of Mists furnished us with wet feet and shrouded us in fog, yet in some way it was delightful. I had the feeling that this was the entrance to something amazing.

The air was not as damp and close as the name of the bridge implied. It was as though the mists became part of us, a magic charm, an illusion created as we crossed over. It was a long bridge, and as our feet glided across the wet planks, the air around us lightened. We held hands so that we wouldn't slip. Titch was right at my side on a short lead.

Suddenly, as if someone had pulled up a blind, or the curtain was rising at the theater, the mist vanished and there was a beautiful view. We were no longer on the bridge, but hovering above golden gravel, glittering in the sunshine beaming down onto the magnificent town of Shamballa. I recognized the towers and pinnacles rising towards the light which flashed from the precious stones used to build the town. It was so lovely it brought tears to my eyes, and I don't even like cities!

My wife covered my eyes with her hands and then stroked my head, from the crown down to my ears, mumbling something the whole time. Another strange transformation took place. The air was full of sound. I could see attractive, shimmering people moving along the same golden road with us, and I could hear them talking to each other in another language. Many had pets with them and they looked and smiled at Titch, who didn't growl, but eyed them slightly suspiciously in return. It was as busy as any city, yet somehow lovely and calm.

"I've directed your thinking and understanding into the fifth dimension," said Sisilla. "You can't stay here with me without becoming part of the whole. Now you'll be able to talk to anybody without even moving your lips. Don't be worried about not understanding the language, as your brain will process it as easily as any other conversation."

She had hardly finished speaking when a young couple stopped us. "We were just admiring your dog," the man said (in my head). "We've never seen that breed before. Where do you come from?" And, hey presto, I only needed to think the answer, and the man understood at once. The woman crouched down to Titch, who licked her hand politely.

"A Great Dane," she echoed with a smile. "We have learned the names of most countries on the surface, and Denmark is no exception. Are the people there especially big?"

I couldn't help laughing, as I thought of the short, good-natured Danes I have met, and all four of us ended up chuckling, and then Titch stood to attention, which caused even more laughter. However, my wife now bade farewell to the couple and we hurried on.

It wasn't long before we had crossed many streets and were by a grand house set in a wonderful garden with a sparkling, woven gate. My wife pressed a button and the gate opened. As we strode along the path of precious stones, I noticed that, while the garden held an array of plants, they were somewhat chaotically displayed. Everything seemed to bloom where it wanted, without design. It was a wild kind of beauty which only Nature can achieve.

We knocked on the great door and heard the latch click open. We entered a massive, roofless hall where leafy branches entwined unimpeded around the walls.

"Welcome to my parents' home!" called my wife, gesturing with arms wide.

The dreaded moment was upon us. There they were: the two people who must be my in-laws. I don't know how they got there; the hall had been empty moments before.

"Kneel!" hissed Sisilla between her teeth. She bowed so low that her wide-brimmed, pink hat fell off. That got a laugh.

Her father raised me up with both hands and looked deep into my eyes. Then he pulled me towards him and welcomed me with a pat on the back. "I can see you're a good man," he said, as I faced him shyly.

Not that I'm usually shy, but he was incredibly impressive. He had the air of a Master, I reflected, without really knowing how a Master would look. He was an upright man with huge charm. His wavy, white hair reached his shoulders and he had a straight mustache and short beard. His eyes were as deep blue as the Atlantic.

"I'm Faio, and you can call me that, as we have no other titles apart from Father and Mother. We'll have some tea and a chat in just a moment, but first I'd like you to meet my wife. Her name's Keeola."

I knelt at once to Sisilla's mother. She was exceedingly pretty, and I could see the similarity to my wife. She wasn't as tall as her husband, and her gleaming, silvery-white hair, piled high on her head, was interlaced with pearls. She wore a white dress and over it a cloak of midnight blue shimmering like the night sky. She commanded respect, but wasn't gentle and friendly like her daughter. Gravely, this austere lady looked me right in the eye and said, "I hope you fulfill our desire for a loving, devoted son-in-law. I like what I see, and bid you welcome. You may kiss my hand!"

She held out a slender, finely-shaped hand with rings on each finger. I kissed it, narrowly avoiding a shiver. She emanated coldness in the same way as my wife emanates warmth.

When I arose, she and Sisilla withdrew, and my father-in-law beckoned me to follow him. We went upstairs and entered a place like an atrium from ancient days. Faio invited me to sit on a sofa.

Although I knew how to create certain products, I don't know how he did it. On the table suddenly a lovely tea set and a plate of sandwiches and cakes appeared.

"Don't be scared of my wife!" He smiled, patting my knee. "Everybody is. She can be offish with strangers, but deep inside, she has a heart of gold."

I had my own opinion about that, but I said nothing. I really liked Faio. "It feels strange to be in the fifth dimension without going through the fourth," I ventured. Faio guffawed.

"Didn't Sisilla explain to you, Tim?" he asked. "She should have, but maybe she couldn't find the right words. You already know about our religion here; we all share the same belief, without exception.

"I have to include the surface in my answer. You know there is about to be a tremendous transformation there.

"Three dimensions encompass height, width, and depth. If we add time to these three, we are into the fourth dimension, where we can consider time from outside.

"Unconsciously — and this is important — people on the surface are passing from the fourth to the fifth dimension, where full consciousness reigns. This goes a long way in explaining people's current confusion — the stress, curious decisions, time that rushes away, karma which is immediately balanced, and so forth.

"The strangest thing of all is that surface-dwellers have the opportunity to progress directly from the third to the fifth dimension. They have been submerged for 13,000 years in the third dimension, manipulated by the Annunaki. The bells of freedom are ringing for them now. The time of reincarnation is past, and life will become part of the Whole.

"According to legend, the Annunaki was a group of Sumerian and Babylonian 'Gods' from the planet Nibiru. Their leader was called Anu. He craved power and wanted to rule the Earth. He planned to enslave the existing population and succeeded beyond expectation, with slavery lasting for thousands of years. He controlled humanity, and managed to convince people *he* was their God.

"The dark forces at his command acted as slaves, and the blossoming, loving Earth, created in the beginning by a different God, was weakened by his tyranny. He prevented distinguished inventors like Tesla and Moray from completing their inventions, by destroying them. He exercised total control over any undesirable development which threatened his power. People were unaware of his existence and influence until recently. Only now is the veil of darkness being torn asunder and light finally penetrating.

"In the third dimension, which we want them to leave, there are opposing energies like good and bad, love and hate, joy and grief, and above all, life and death. In higher dimensions these don't exist. Your controlling ego no longer dominates your world. Instead, the Higher Self takes over, and the Creation and the Unity dominate in everyone. In short, the fourth dimension is the astral plane, populated by ghosts and specters."

I was overwhelmed. I just about managed to say 'thank you,' and my father-in-law smiled indulgently.

"For those who have lived on the surface most of their lives, this is strange news indeed, whereas we have been aware of this since childhood. We need to be able to explain to Earthlings where they are when they get here. They can forget all about the fourth dimension. It has a certain type of clientele, and some Earthlings may choose to move there. That is their business. There is still free will on Earth. We will assist those who wish it. We take into account the choice of the individual."

128

"What a job!" I groaned.

"There are many of us," my father-in-law said, smiling, "a great many; and we will achieve our goal. You've already noticed that Agartha is a pleasant place to live, free from toxins and evil."

"So the fourth dimension is the astral world," I mumbled.

"Yes, and now you know, you've no need to dwell on it any further. We have other things to discuss: your immediate duty here, for instance. Have you decided what work you will do?"

"Aren't I going to be some kind of liaison between Agartha and the surface?" I suggested uncertainly.

"It just so happens that I am chairman of the Great Circle here in Shamballa, and as my son-in-law, you are entitled to a position among us. Of course, this is your choice, but we would not appreciate you commuting between the surface and Sisilla, who would be left on her own. It would be better for you to stay here and make your home in Shamballa or somewhere nearby."

"What would the job involve?" I inquired, quaking inwardly. Would I have to leave Grandmother and my friends in Telos? Didn't I already have work there with Mannul?

"As you are well acquainted with the Earth's surface, its inhabitants, its history, and its countries, your mission here would be as Earth's ambassador, as you call it. You would partake in all things pertaining to the Earth! What do you think?"

"It sounds just like what Mannul suggested recently, but without the incessant travel," I cried in delight. "I accept without hesitation!"

"Then that's all arranged." My father-in-law patted my shoulder in contentment. "It means you don't have to travel to the surface — at least, only occasionally. You may live where you want, but your office will naturally be in Telos, as surface-dwellers tend to arrive there first. There will be problems to solve. You'll interview Earthlings and assess their suitability for immigration. You are welcome to have an assistant, as you will certainly need one."

"May I have Mannul?" I asked eagerly, and my father-in-law agreed at once.

"I am on a study trip just at the moment," I continued. "What should we do about that?"

"Carry on! You need to learn as much as you can," replied Faio. "Then we'll initiate you into the fifth dimension. That's an obvious stipulation for this kind of work. Hello, ladies!"

My mother-in-law and wife appeared suddenly out of nowhere. They were both very cheerful and I noticed that my mother-in-law's laugh rang out as happily as my wife's. She came and gave me a big hug, at last.

"We have to go home," Sisilla announced, "because we are about to receive VIPs from the surface. You and I must welcome Cardinal Reimfort from the Vatican!"

The hovercraft was waiting at the door, and we bid each other a hasty farewell. Titch seemed very relieved to be going home. His charm hadn't been fully appreciated in this place, so he licked any part of me he could find and flopped down beside me in the vehicle with a deep sigh.

24. The Cardinal from the Vatican

"Congratulations! Your new job starts now, with a celebrity from the Vatican," my wife teased, as we alighted from the hovercraft. Mannul was waiting at home for us, with Valencio and a well-groomed man of medium height in a suit. I realized this must be Cardinal Reimfort.

It crossed my mind that I ought to genuflect. I scanned his face, which was gentle and friendly, pale, with a slightly prominent nose, and expressive eyes. There were finely-drawn lines around his eyes and mouth. His head was clean-shaven, apart from a ring of graying hair on his crown. He seemed very pleasant. He was wearing a mauve shirt and a well-tailored suit of gray. I didn't have time to kneel. As a non-Catholic, it's a difficult decision. To my surprise, he knelt elegantly and kissed my hand. Good grief, I thought, falling back on my grandmother's expression, is the man mad?

"Thank you!" he cried in faultless English, rising swiftly. "I am most grateful to you for looking after my ward, Valencio. I guessed as soon as he disappeared that he would come here, as I had just told him about Agartha, never having been here myself. When I was young, before I became a prelate, I met a sailor who recounted stories about your country, and I have always wanted to visit. The Pope gave me the task of finding the boy and asking him to return. The Pope can never openly acknowledge his paternity, but I can help Valencio, if he wants to come home. I have tried to be a father to him since he was born. Valencio would be brought up as a cardinal, but we will respect his wishes."

I took the old gentleman's arm and led him into the house. My wife managed to produce a cup of strong coffee, which the prelate drank with pleasure.

"Would Your Eminence care to see more of this country inside the

Earth?" I asked, still shaken that the old priest had knelt to me. Titch sniffed at the Cardinal, licked his hand, and sat down beside him. As usual, my sensible dog demonstrated his positive feelings.

"Thank you, I would like that!" Reimfort nodded and smiled. "It would be delightful. I may wish to stay! The inner workings of the Vatican are becoming too much for me. My son is here, and has already expressed a desire to remain here. And, as far as I understand, you believe in the same God, don't you?"

Sisilla replied, "The light of the Creator derives from the inexhaustible Source, the Source of Life. We live in unison with the Source, the Light, and each other. Together, these represent God's Love for us."

"Hmm," said the Cardinal thoughtfully. "I've never heard it put like that before, but it sounds fine. I can agree with that without any qualms. I'm grateful to be allowed to stay here a few days and get to know you better, with Valencio, or Val as I usually call him."

"I can undertake to show your Eminence around," said Mannul, who had been as quiet as a mouse until now, sitting beside the prelate. "We have priests who can elaborate on our spiritual philosophy. And anyway, you should experience our wonderful countryside. There's a good guest house in Telos where you could stay."

"If I could stay with Valencio, then I would happily accept!" The Cardinal rose, bowing first to my wife and then to me. He accompanied Mannul to the hovercraft.

"He'll want to stay here!" remarked my wife with satisfaction. "What a nice man!"

I hurried to Grandmother with news of the visit. She and her new husband Lex were eating lunch in the garden when I turned up. Grandmother hugged me.

"My dear boy," she exclaimed. "I was beginning to wonder where you'd got to. We've been to some very exciting places, including a botanical garden with plants from the surface. Imagine that! There were colt's foot, blue anemones, lilies of the valley, and many more of my favorites."

I told them about the Pope's son and his guardian, the Cardinal, meeting up here, and that the Cardinal was considering staying. Grandmother was jubilant.

"What lovely people there are here!" she laughed. "We must throw a party. I have to meet a real cardinal. I would like to tell him what religion is really about."

Lex and I exchanged glances. Neither of us planned to let Grandmother loose.

"The Wesak celebrations are upon us," Lex observed. "Apparently, it's a holiday we share with the surface. It's a celebration of the birth of the Buddha and his enlightenment, a tribute to the Light."

"Never heard of it," I replied. "It's completely passed me by up there and down here. Pretty much like God. How do the two Gods compare?"

"By being exactly the same," replied Lex dryly. "There's no difference at all. We are surrounded by the Great Spirit and the Source, united in an indivisible whole, the Unity."

"I've never been very involved in religion," I confessed, slightly embarrassed. "I didn't realize they had a proper religion here."

"Let's call it belief," Lex pointed out. "The concept of 'religion' is over-used, and isn't used here."

"I wonder where education takes place here, especially higher education," said Grandmother. "I know that small children learn in Porthologos, but there must be other types of education, and even vocational training."

"There is," I replied. "There are centers of education, like our universities, all over the place."

"Great," exclaimed Grandmother. "I was thinking of Valencio. It wouldn't do him any harm to continue his studies. I'm sure it's fine to be conversant with Armenian, Latin, and other ancient languages, but he needs licking into shape, as well as general knowledge about the surface and the fifth dimension, which Lex and I are working on. You know I've always been interested in magic, and white magic is five-dimensional."

"Actually, that's what I'm learning with Mannul," I concurred. "I'm learning from him and an old fellow called Arniel."

Grandmother laughed. "They're obviously not teaching you humility," she remarked. "But maybe that will come later when you are five-dimensional."

"I'm partly there already," I replied, sulking a little. "I am married to a five-dimensional woman." To my grandmother's delight, I recounted the story of our visit to Sisilla's parents.

Lex told me I had become part of a family with ancient roots and traditions, and that it would be just as well if I hurried home to celebrate. I bade them a hasty farewell. I had to look after the Cardinal and accompany my wife to the festivities. Maybe I could combine both things.

25. Festivities in Agartha

The Cardinal, Valencio, and my friend Mannul were all in the living room waiting for me. Mannul rushed over to embrace me.

"I've ordered us a hovercraft," he declared. "We're going to show Cardinal Reimfort one of our finest traditions. I think he'll be impressed." This last sentence he whispered in my ear with a big smile. I looked at the Cardinal. He was in full clerical garb, complete with a funny, little, tasseled hat, and a purple silk hood covered in embroidery. I bowed low to the venerable vision. He gave me a friendly smile.

"I don't know where we're going," he said, "so it's just as well if people can see who I am."

"Clerical clothes may not be of any interest in this country," Mannul observed gently, "but Your Eminence looks so elegant, it would be a shame not to show off these wonderful vestments."

Val, as we now called Valencio, looked a bit embarrassed. His white jeans were dirty and his blue checked shirt crumpled. He had been playing with the children and hadn't had time to change. My wife came to the rescue. She produced a perfect white suit, silk shirt, and a tie, and presented them to him.

"There." She smiled. "I'm sure they'll fit. There's no shortage of clothes here. You can change in the bedroom. Tim is going to change, too. I've laid out his clothes on the bed. Go on, off you go, you two!"

I was to wear the traditional Agarthan "folk costume": shimmering natural silk trousers, a beautiful embroidered shirt with inset stones, and an exquisite, broad belt with bejeweled embroidery. These belts are worth mentioning: skilfully executed gold squares with a multitude of precious stones illustrating images from Agartha's history. They also indicate the history of the wearer.

"I don't feel great," whispered Val as we changed. "Uncle Luigi, the Cardinal, wants me to return to the Vatican with him, and he's really stubborn. He won't budge."

"But he said he wanted to stay!" I burst out in surprise. "Has he changed his mind?"

"He was just pretending, to keep me happy. Oh, please help me! I don't want to go back. I want to stay and make a future for myself here." He stopped talking as the Cardinal came in with Mannul.

"We're going now! Hurry up! Emilie and her husband are coming with us, as they're not sure where we're going. There's a party venue, you see. Come on!"

We ran swiftly out of the house and jumped into the hovercraft with a boisterous dog. Titch took up a lot of room, but I couldn't deny him the trip.

The celebration area was enormous. I can't do it justice with a description, as you couldn't see from one end to the other, and it was filled to overflowing with milling people. It was like a huge bowl of rice pudding, as most people were dressed in white, and many women had white headscarves. These scarves were braided imaginatively and sparkled with jewels. I have never seen the like, or imagined anything as amazing.

In the middle of the crowd was a circular arena like a circus. As we arrived, a path opened up through the throng, and people bowed and waved.

"Why are we allowed through?" I whispered to Sisilla.

"They can see your belt," she replied. "Only people who work on the Council have a belt like that."

I had had no idea. Questions filled my head as we were led to the arena and invited to be seated. Sisilla's parents were there, to my surprise, and many faces I recognized from my field-trip to the Council chamber.

Arniel appeared and welcomed us all. "We always have a major meeting at Wesak," he explained. "Everyone comes who can, as there will be songs, speeches, and plays."

I looked around. We were sitting in a ring on plump, white sofas, around a large empty area in the middle. Suddenly, there was a man on a gilded podium. He had light-brown hair and beard and the most clear dark-blue eyes I've ever seen. He smiled, radiating Love and beauty.

"My beloved citizens, sisters and brothers!" he called. "We are gathered here this evening to celebrate the Love of the Light and the Source, as we usually do. May all facets of the Light be within us and be a glowing connection with God …"

Here the prelate from the Vatican stood up and in a voice of thunder called, "… and Jesus Christ, the only son of God!"

The man on the podium turned his bearded face towards the Cardinal. Smiling, he remarked, "You're new here, aren't you? Otherwise you'd know that I'm Jesus, known as Christ on the surface, and I'm one of the Masters of Shamballa. None of us wants to claim to be the only son or any other distinction. Nobody prays to us. The only one who lights up heaven is God, who reigns supreme and is the Source of all Creation. For us, there is only one."

"Blasphemy!" bellowed the Cardinal, bright red in the face. "I don't believe for one moment that you are Jesus Christ. As if he would be underground talking to every Tom, Dick, and Harry! You are blaspheming against everything which is holy by posing as the son of God."

"That was your suggestion, not mine." There was an icy edge to Jesus' voice now. "Would you recognize a physical manifestation of Jesus? I'm afraid you're in troubled waters, my friend. Everyone here knows I'm Jesus, Saint Germain is Saint Germain, and Melchizedek is Melchizedek, and that we, and many others who are Masters, exist in the fifth dimension in Shamballa."

"Oh sure!" raged the prelate, getting angrier. "If you lived there, you'd be over two thousand years old!

"You're all liars! The worst thing is that the whole populace seems to believe your fanciful assertions!" He swung his head angrily so that the small cap with the large tassel arrangement ended up perched rakishly over one ear. The audience roared with laughter and we joined in. Val went and pulled his uncle by the arm.

"Come on, Uncle Luigi, there's no point in this!"

"We're going home tomorrow," hissed the Cardinal, "and you are coming too, if I have to carry you. I had no idea that the renowned paradise of Shamballa was a den of swindlers and rogues. I should never have come. I'm glad to have found you, my son. Now you'll return with me and read for the priesthood. I'm sure the Pope has a fine position up his sleeve for you."

"Really." Val was seething with barely concealed anger. "If you think I'm going to take up some sham position, you're a misguided bunch in the Vatican. I'm not coming. I'm staying here."

"We'll see about that," said the Cardinal in a tone of superiority. I heard this exchange and decided the boy needed support. Jesus stepped down from the podium and my whisper to him left him grinning from ear to ear. He nodded in affirmation.

The Cardinal was looking grim. He was dragging a reluctant Val by the arm, trying to forge a path through the crowd. He hadn't learned to hover, and people were moving aside with cheerful shouts and friendly pats on his embroidered shoulder.

A lovely, lively, red-headed young girl took the liberty of rearranging the Cardinal's cap and waved to Val. "Here's someone who wants to meet you!" she said. "It's important, and work-related."

"He's going nowhere," mumbled the Cardinal. "He's going back to the hotel in this God-forsaken country."

The girl, however, put her hand upon his, which was holding Valencio in a grip of iron. The priest's fingers relinquished Valencio's sleeve, and our highly-esteemed prelate began to disappear. In a moment, the Cardinal and his dazzling outfit had completely vanished. Jesus and I were standing a short way off with a surprised Italian boy.

"The Cardinal is back in the Vatican," Jesus explained. "I sent him home, as his behavior was not conducive to our festive blessing. Would you like to go with Cardinal Reimfort, Valencio?"

Valencio shook his head vigorously. He had grasped the red-headed girl's hand, and Titch, despite the crush, was trying to jump up and climb on them. Jesus climbed back onto the podium, laughing, and waved to an invisible orchestra, which commenced a wonderful melody. People danced where they could, mostly with their feet on the ground and arms around each other, swaying to the beat. An exceedingly beautiful rainbow became the background for an energetic song. I watched the two young people obviously getting acquainted.

Val looked at the girl, and she looked at him. I remembered meeting Sisilla for the first time; that was also at a dance.

"That's Arniel's daughter!" someone whispered in my ear. "Her name's Tiira. She'll look after Val, don't worry!"

It was Mannul who had caught me up. Titch had found me straight away, of course. We returned to the white sofa next to the podium.

The rest of the evening was like a dream. I thought there would be lots of boring speeches, but there weren't! Wall to wall songs and dances of a quality the Metropolitan would've envied. It's difficult to find words to describe that night. I held my wife's hand, Grandmother held Lex's, and Val held Tiira's. We were provided delicious food and cakes, and drank the typical Agarthan wine. The crowds thinned as the evening progressed, and we enjoyed everything. The air was pleasantly warm and heavy with the aroma of flowers and herbs. Enough to make one doze off …

26. Visiting an Agarthan Orphanage

Val didn't appear to miss his guardian. He often came around to chat and to drink tea. Sometimes Tiira came with him. She turned out to be a singer and actor and a very happy, kind girl. There was definitely something between them. I wished them luck with all my heart.

Some days later, I was in the garden early one morning. Sisilla was still asleep and I was in the arbor listening to the birds. Titch was with me, of course. I reflected on all I'd seen since the awful shipwreck and losing my father. I thought back to the training here in Telos and meeting my dear Sisilla.

I considered all the new friends and new experiences here, and felt happy and grateful that I was still me — a little wiser possibly — and not cold and dead on the sea-bed. Another life had awaited me, in a different place, in another dimension.

Actually, I have never felt as alive as I do here and now.

Mannul and Valencio came to collect me for the day's lesson. Sitting in the hovercraft, Val enquired, "I think about angels sometimes and wonder if there are angels here, and if not, where are they? Are we angels, even though we think we are alive? Some people do become angels, like the holy Madonna and the saints, don't they?"

"You have to stop thinking like a Catholic!" Mannul scolded him. "There is no religion here, just a belief in the infinite Creator. Angels are a race in the fifth dimension, not dead people who have been transformed. That idea is completely erroneous, although I know many surface-dwellers believe it. They hope to become angels when they die. That is not how it works. Angels are certainly incredibly helpful, good beings who are responsible for helping humans. They walk between dimensions and are very wise and sensible. The Bible, which mentions angels, is a book like any other, a mixture of imagination and unverified history which surface-dwellers have decided to put on a pedestal and worship. Not everything in it is true. Not all an author writes is true."

* * *

"Excuse me, Mariana, we don't mean you!" Tim remarked, smiling. "What is written in this book and what I'm conveying to you is actually true. The surface-dwellers need to know that we really exist! We'll provide physical proof soon, but I don't know when. It will happen! We'll come back to that later."

* * *

"Will I be able to meet an angel?" asked Val.

"Perhaps," replied Mannul. "It all depends on you. You have a lot to learn first."

"As you know by now, there's not only life on Earth," I interjected. "There are different forms of life across the whole Universe, and basic human life is similar, even if the Creator gave it slightly varied forms. There is human life, if I may call it that, on many planets other than Earth."

This was difficult for a newcomer like Val to grasp, and I could relate to that. I had seen so much evidence to back up my claims, that there was no doubt left in my mind. He was silent now, but he'd soon see proof.

The hovercraft stopped. From a large, round building of gemstones a crowd of children flowed forth. They boarded the hovercraft and threw themselves at us. They kissed us and hugged us and patted us where they could. Mannul burst out laughing. "I wanted to show you an orphanage in Telos," he said, grinning. "This is the ultimate hands-on experience! Calm down, kids, and we'll get out."

The children retreated quickly; a group of happy, noisy completely normal children.

"I wanted to show you an Agarthan orphanage," he resumed. "It might be less rowdy now. Come on in!"

For once, Titch seemed subdued. There were children swarming all over him. He knew he was too large for even the tallest child to pet his back, and realized that it would be best to lie down. I could only make out his black nose, which emanated resignation, and I had to laugh. Soon he managed to escape from the attention, and padded along with us, close by my side.

It is difficult for a surface-dweller to imagine an orphanage like this. I reflected that the children must be happy here.

Each one of them had a space of their own with a bed, chest of drawers, and chairs. The assembly hall was huge, with all kinds of musical instruments in it, a climbing frame, and floor-cushions. A little boy came and patted my cheek.

"Someone puts us to bed each night," he told me. "They tell us a story and hug and kiss us goodnight. If anyone is upset, they are comforted and hugged more. We get good food and lots of tooth-friendly sweets. Ill children get better very quickly. Somebody always comes to make us better."

There was plenty of time for Love here. These little children were brought up in a loving atmosphere and encouraged to respond lovingly. It was a wonderful, liberating feeling seeing these orphans growing up surrounded by Love.

"Sometimes children come here from the surface too," Mannul told us. "Sometimes we collect children who are having difficulties on the surface. They are registered as 'disappeared' and nobody even looks for them."

Val sighed and said, "If they had only looked after me like this! I'd like to work in this amazing place."

We were back in the hovercraft.

I had begun to realize how important positive thinking is; not just going with the flow. The power of thought is our strongest weapon and our strongest defense and our only opportunity for creativity — and I mean CREATIVITY. It took a long time before I learned to live by thinking, and creating through thought. Without Sisilla, I don't know how I would've coped with all the education. In a strange, mystical way, knowledge stayed in my head instead of going in one ear and out the other. My memory was reliable, and I learned to increase it in various ways. There was plenty to remember in my new life at this time of change.

The next stop was a temple. We were to survey the everyday lives of priests and priestesses, Mannul explained. I had already done this.

"Priests and priestesses always work in pairs here," he continued. "Often married couples take on difficult cases."

"What does 'difficult' entail?" Val's question was fairly obvious.

"Love isn't always as pure as it should be," was Mannul's cryptic reply. "People have emotional problems here. When difficulties arise, there's always the clergy to talk to, and solutions are found to all problems."

As we didn't have any great problems, it was mostly a guided tour of the inner temple, which was beautifully decorated with flowers. I noticed that Val stole up to the altar, crossed himself, and clasped his hands. A persistent seed had been planted in the dark rooms of the Vatican.

There wasn't really an altar in the normal sense. There were lovely paintings and a small podium where the two priests were sitting. There were plenty of beautifully arranged flowers. Elementals were fluttering around inside and outside, and the color, perfume, and music contributed to the atmosphere of peace.

"How old can you get here?" asked Val. "Someone suggested hundreds of years, but I can't believe that. He said you look young forever. That's mad!"

Mannul grinned broadly at him. "But it's true. The food we eat and the life we live are compatible with the highest principles of LIFE. It's a secret you surface-dwellers have never been able to understand."

"Isn't it boring to live so long?" Val's face reflected the suspicion and scepticism which I had felt myself when I first came.

I understood him, so I answered, "No, it never gets boring. Four hours of work and four singing, dancing, and playing, fill the days faster than you can imagine. The tiredness you feel at the end of the day is natural and healthy and makes for a wonderful sleep. I haven't felt bored since I got here."

"I asked Tiira too, but she just laughed. She didn't seem to understand the question," said Val glumly. "I'm going to try to believe you, and I've definitely decided to stay here. I want to see more; I want to see everything!"

Mannul and I exchanged glances and grinned. This boy was shaping up well, and the thought of him destined for priesthood at the Vatican made me shiver.

Our hovercraft flew around with us to the airport, the woods, the sea, and small villages. High up in the mountains, gemstone processing took place, polishing and design. Val was like a schoolboy, hanging around the various craftsmen and eating noisily, with obvious delight, the vegetarian food we supplied him with.

When we finally came to a stop by the elegant entrance to Porthologos, Mannul exclaimed, "Now I've shown you life in Telos and its vicinity. It's time for you to learn how to use the power of thought to create what you want, as long as it's positive."

"What about the fifth dimension?" Val wondered. "When will I experience that?"

"Not today, anyway!" chuckled Mannul. "I'm glad you're eager to learn, and in due course you will learn everything. Now we're going into the library for a lesson in the art of creating, for which you will have the best teacher: Arniel."

Val jumped, and put his hands to his mouth as if to stifle a yelp. Instead he whimpered, "Oh dear! Tiira's dad! Is there a men's room where I can make myself presentable?"

27. How the Earth Will Change

I sat contentedly the whole way home. It had been a wonderful, if tiring, day, and Titch slept with his head on my lap while I yawned prodigiously. At home, good food awaited me and an affectionate wife, who listened patiently to all I had to recount. She had plenty to talk about, too.

When she'd finished, the doorbell rang and a man I'd never met before entered before we could open the door. I guess he was human, because that's how he appeared. But you never know …!

He sort of glowed. He was tall, but they all are here. He was wearing a shimmering silver cape and a wide, embroidered belt. He had dark, shoulder-length, curly hair and a face that was attractive, but not particularly youthful. His nose was prominent, but shapely. His eyes glittered like jewels. You felt privileged to be on the receiving end of his smile. He stretched out his arms and hugged my wife and then me. The hug was like electricity which left you devoid of anything other than an obvious, gentle NOW.

"I'm Alberto Abertas," he announced.

My wife added, "The wisest man in the whole of Agartha!"

"I've come because you're writing a book about our part of the planet Earth," he continued, sitting down in a chair.

"My other name means Opening. I work alongside the Count Saint Germain and Master Hilarion. I know Sisilla's parents, and want to congratulate you on your Love Union. I also want to discuss the plans we have for the future of the planet, in the limelight at present. Surface-dwellers have no idea what to expect, and we need to inform them."

"I realize something has to be done," I nodded in agreement. "Neighboring planets are beginning to feel the effects on the atmosphere caused by the surface-dwellers — poisoning, treachery, and suchlike."

"Development on the surface has been too negative," agreed our guest. "The whole galaxy is on standby. We have worked long and hard to banish the forces of evil, and we have been fairly successful. It's time to increase these Earthly energies. I've come to prepare you to warn the surface-dwellers about what will soon happen. You have an important role in this context, Tim, as you are the leader for surface-dwellers who come here accidentally. They don't have perception of the problems, and these are numerous.

"We are going to discuss density. Within physics there are various kinds of density. People have one kind of density, whereas other worlds normally have a lighter density. Our spaceship and what you call spirits and ghosts, for example, have the ability of appearing invisible to you. You have no idea of the invisible life around you.

"Planet Earth has Free Will to play with. I use the word 'play' advisedly, as we use free will in many negative ways. On other planets free will is limited and held in check. Violence and egotism aren't allowed. Your will has developed in the wrong direction. You use it for evil, and call on powers which shouldn't be allowed to exist.

"The whole galaxy unanimously believes it is time for the Earth to restructure in a positive way. At this point in time, the work has already commenced. It is high time to cleanse your beautiful planet of all the rubbish which is threatening to suffocate it and Mother Earth. We are going to do this soon."

"What are you going to do?" I asked. "Is there really a chance of saving Earth?"

"Yes!" His answer echoed in the clear evening air and felt like a sword thrust into all nooks and crannies. He continued, "We will make sure that all your weapons crumble so they can never be used again. Rage and aggression are concepts and feelings which must be banished. You have to realize that these symbols of evil have no place in the world of Love which will rule on Earth. Violence must end NOW.

"We advise you to live peacefully and spiritually. Your reward for this is to automatically reach a higher level of life. You will have to teach your children at an early stage not to hurt each other and to treat others as they wish to be treated themselves. You will have to practice thinking kind thoughts and being kind. The same goes for your governments. We're already in the process of trying to achieve honest and effective actions in the name of humanity. Stop competing; it's not a race!

"Very soon, the whole planet will be evacuated. The Earth will move into the fifth dimension and the surface will be purified. As the Earth's frequency increases, electricity will cease to function. There will be mass landings of the Galactic Federation's lightships in towns and the countryside in all countries. All those alive will be taken into the ships. We will divide up the negative and positive souls, the three-dimensional and the five-dimensional, and there will be a great reformation of human souls on Earth.

"Once you are in the ships, you will be able to witness the transformation of Earth. It will be a fantastic sight. You will come to know things which have been cosmic secrets."

"I think I'm going to faint," I groaned. "Now I realize why I'm here and what I have to do. Many people from above will end up here, right?"

"Exactly." Our new friend smiled. "Both you and Sisilla will coordinate with the refugees. The new Earth will be expanded to five-dimensional on the inside and the outside. The deserts will disappear and instead there will be tropical paradises.

"The inside and the surface will be reunited. There will be plenty of World Trees. Enter one of these, and you enter a beautiful extension of the Earth …"

"I didn't understand that bit," I interrupted in confusion. "The trees will have a different environment inside? Are you joking?"

"You might think so," laughed Alberto. "Lots of things will happen, but it is too soon to discuss them now, as your form is very physical. That will also change. Do you realize that you will be able to see and work with elementals?"

"Absolutely! We're already friends, as is my dog, Titch."

"Animals see them and regret that you can't. But Mother Earth is eager to transform and take on a new guise not destroyed by human economic transactions, their toxins, and egotistical felling of forests, crucial to wildlife and oxygen-production.

"You should know that our technology is light years ahead of yours. We will share our knowledge when the time is ripe. There will be many alternatives in communication and entertainment. Each household will be supplied with a machine which transforms light energy into matter. It will provide you with clothes and food. There will be prosperity programs which will provide the financial resources necessary. None of this can be revealed in detail before notification of the first wave of changes.

"You will have new methods of transportation, making cars, trains, and airplanes obsolete. Great changes await transport and infrastructure. New technology will transform medicine. Our technology will reverse the terrible pollution surrounding you. Your entire environment will change fast.

"There will be no wars. People are brothers and sisters across the world. You will be able to travel across the universe. There will be complete inter-galactic co-operation.

"This is just a fraction of your immediate future. Sisilla and Timothy, you must both understand that your powers will be used to the utmost in this amazing transformation, which has been planned by the Galactic Council for thousands of years. I have to leave now, but I will return, as we're part of a group who will coordinate on various missions here and on Earth."

As quickly as he had come, Master Alberto Abertas, creator of this new epoch, vanished. I sat as if stunned, until my wife hugged me. Her face was streaked with tears of happiness.

"We're the chosen ones who will help the Earth back into the fold of the Creator — the Great Spirit, which is the Cosmic Source of the Universe," she sniffed. I was glad that I would be able to tell Grandmother and her husband next morning. They were bound to have a mission, too, in this changing world.

28. Indian Wisdom and the Fire of Life

Valencio knocked on my door. He appeared totally elated. Mannul was behind him, smiling from ear to ear. I've never seen anyone else do this, but he was expert at it.

"It's going to be an exciting day!" exclaimed Val. "We're going to meet Indians!"

"Let me go first, boy!" Mannul scolded. "I'll explain." He sat down with me and my wife. Val initiated a hugging session with Titch.

"Indians have lived in Agartha since the formation of the continent," Mannul told us. "You've just met one of them, Alberto Abertas, a man you will meet again soon. Indian culture is as old as time and has been appreciated here most of all. Most Indians are five-dimensional. A very few, those who have only just arrived, are three-dimensional. The ones who have lived here down the ages are considered the wisest of all.

"We have secret contact with some present-day tribes. They have entrances from above and tunnels connecting Peru and elsewhere. They have a wonderful communications network. They are considered traditionalists in Agartha.

"Their wisdom is infinite, their Love unconditional, and their culture the best preserved of all. There is one problem: They are suspicious of strangers. That's why Alberto and I are coming, too. If he wasn't with us, they wouldn't let us in. They have suffered such humiliation from the surface that you need reliable references to be allowed into their kingdom. Forget you are the Pope's son, Val. It's considered a disadvantage!"

"I've always loved Indians," objected Val enthusiastically. "I read tons of Indian books when I was small, and I've always thought they were badly treated."

"And are still," I added. "I'm glad to be meeting them."

"There are no class conflicts here," Mannul continued. "We are all equal in the face of the Father. But they don't want bad vibes from surface-dwellers. That's happened too often. It won't be a problem if we arrive with Alberto. He'll be here any moment."

Here we don't generally use expressions of time like "any minute," as Agarthans don't live by the clock, but by the signs of Nature. But it was only a few minutes before Alberto knocked, and we entered the hovercraft waiting outside. "Enter" is a good word, although "embark" would do just as well, as you climb three steep steps to get into one of these vehicles, which otherwise looks like an open car without wheels.

Titch was used to it now, and he was the first one in, sitting in the front, leaving a tiny space for me. Sisilla stayed home, maintaining that she was busy. In actual fact, at my urgent request, she was going to see how the land lay for Val. He was thinking of getting married and was pining for the red-headed madcap, Tiira. Sisilla had known Tiira's parents from childhood.

The way to Indian country was long, but the loveliness I experienced was nearly devastating. There were no deserts or overgrown wildernesses. The land was cultivated, with regular places for rest and meditation. I've never seen so many varieties of flowers as in Agartha. Mannul explained that the profusion of flowers was part of the kingdom's root system. It helped to clean the air, achieving positive energy with its perfumed message and contributing to the inhabitants' well-being.

We landed gently. I looked around before Titch pulled impatiently at my sleeve to get out. The air was as balmy as Mannul had promised, and the landscape a romantic dream. There were no barriers, just endless mountains, lakes, and tall trees, many in blossom. I could see no compact buildings, just wicker walls entwined with plants. Alberto stepped out of the other hovercraft and welcomed us warmly to his region of Agartha.

It was truly lovely.

There was an occasional totem pole. These were made of precious stones and weren't exactly like the ones on the surface. The play of sunlight on the multitude of beautifully-polished stones was blinding. Around them, also decorated in stones, was semi-circular seating with cushions. Alberto explained that people would sit here to meditate. Nothing but the True God was worshiped, the Source of all creation.

"Here's the Fire of Life!" announced Alberto, indicating a winding path. We followed the path and soon found ourselves on a hillside. Above us, at the top of the hill, there was a building that gleamed so brightly it hurt our eyes to look at it.

"The Fire of Life restores youth and vitality to the visitor," explained Mannul. "It bestows upon him great clarity of thought and deed, removing any trace of illness and filling him with joie de vivre. All people should be cleansed by it, but that is unfortunately not possible. The Powers that be make those decisions."

I thought of Grandmother and the stories she had told me when I was small, visiting Sweden, about a holy fire that restored youth and happiness. Here it was! I also knew that there was a room in Telos where youth and vigor could be restored. It was obviously considered important in this strange land.

Our health is of paramount importance. Without it we are pitiful craft floating on the ocean of life. On the surface we have doctors and hospitals, but I prefer the health centers of Agartha. Mannul informed us that all tribes and villages had similar places. Illness contributed to economic markets on Earth, and was completely unnecessary. We would be able to show them later how to heal.

Alberto Abertas led us through the peculiar, intertwined village so that I could study its strange construction. There were no castles or manor houses, just round or straight walls glimpsed through overwhelmingly luxuriant foliage. Houses are somewhere to live for us. Here they are incredible constructions, alive with people. We saw people everywhere in gaudy, colorful costumes. They were either running around or busy with old-fashioned jobs.

Alberto noticed my confusion, but Valencio anticipated my questions by asking, "How do these people make a living? Are there no factories to produce goods they need? To me, this feels like going back hundreds of years."

"You should know by now that we create all we need," replied Mannul abruptly. "We still make our own remedies and cures. Children fall down even here, and people get stomach-aches, toothaches, and headaches. Accidents happen and we get hurt just like you. We have medicine for everything. The people here are making herbal remedies, collecting herbs and roots in the forests."

"Do the aborigines do the same?" Val asked.

"Pretty much," Alberto answered. "We have our own traditions. All tribes, whatever the name, have their own culture, but we share the same god, the Source, the Creator, the Word of Love which was the Word in the beginning."

"Do you have similar places of worship?" It was my turn to ask questions.

"The various cultures have intentionally diverse places of worship," replied Alberto. "People have to feel comfortable in their belief, even if the beliefs are compatible. We respect people's differences. If problems arise, we solve them."

"You always say that!" I protested. "Always can be such an uncertain term. Is there someone to turn to if a problem arises, or are the tears shed inwardly in silence?"

"Old Mother Sjaluna is life's servant," replied Alberto. "We'll look in on her and you'll get a better answer than I can give you."

In a glade beside a huge rock, a woman was sitting on the grass by a fire. She was stirring a cauldron and tasting its contents from time to time. She was small and so thin that her ribs protruded, and her pale face was so wrinkled that there was hardly room for her eyes, nose, and mouth. You would have expected wisps of hair, but to my surprise, I was completely wrong. Old Mother Sjaluna had a mane a lion would have envied! She had gleaming, black hair with curls around her face.

She was quite a sight, and she sounded more like a crowing magpie than a human when she spoke. And yet, her words were as clear as embroidery on an otherwise blank canvas. She looked at each of us in turn, and I could feel her gaze was more intense than you would suppose.

"To what do I owe the pleasure of a visit from fine, healthy folk?" she asked, continuing to stir her brew. "I'm busy with a cure for the sick: for those who have lost their way from God. They crawl around like lice on a bronze statue. You don't look lost!"

Alberto leaned over and whispered in her ear. He was rewarded with a toothless smile and a nod. She removed her hand momentarily from the ladle and pointed with a claw-like nail over her left shoulder. We followed Alberto through branches concealing a hole in a great boulder. It was the entrance to a cave.

I was again greeted by a sight I was unprepared for. Val grasped my shoulder and whispered, "What is that?"

29. Old Mother Sjaluna's Gift

We were in quite a roomy cavern, tastefully furnished with seating around a high bench. A restful light pervaded in dull colors. Meditation music played softly in the background. There were arm chairs, obviously intended for the "therapist" and "patient." The old lady was suddenly sitting in one of the chairs. How she had gotten there was a mystery.

"Is that the patient?" she asked, pointing to Val. Titch had crept shamelessly to her side. Her hand, previously so busy stirring, now stroked my dog softly.

"If the boy will sit with me a moment, I'll sort out the mess in his head," Old Mother Sjaluna chirped. "He's madly in love, which makes it more difficult."

Val sat down reluctantly in the armchair opposite her. Suddenly, the old lady smiled, and her gnarled hands gripped Val's fists.

"That'll have to wait, anyway," she announced, grinning. I realized all of a sudden how much the smile lit up her old face, so that it exuded Love and no longer appeared so ancient. "It won't be as easy as he thinks, but it will happen in the end! The young puppy will grow into a fine fellow! But don't give up! Don't let anyone else meddle in your life, as that will be your downfall!"

Valencio didn't dare say a word. He seemed subdued, but not scared. "Can't … can't I marry the one I love?" Val asked querulously. The old lady burst out laughing.

"The young rascal wants a woman!" she exclaimed. "But didn't he hear what I said? Not yet. It will happen in due course. Here, now is always now. It can only be like that until the next now is ready. He has to understand that if he's staying!"

And with that cryptic reply he had to be satisfied. As he got up, the old lady seized his arm. "Don't be in such a hurry. Make haste slowly. Play first before you settle down!"

True to his upbringing, the Pope's son politely kissed her hand. Old Mother Sjaluna was surprised and delighted. Then she pointed at me.

"Come to me, Sisilla's husband. I have something for you."

She was still stroking Titch's neck, which he was enjoying to no end.

"Sit down!" she ordered, as though I were a dog. I did so. "Shut your eyes," she commanded, and I did that too.

I felt two fingers vibrating on my eyelids and tremendous warmth.

"Timothy needs to be able to see more," she explained.

"He's married into one of our best families, and he has to be able to keep up! He didn't have the gift, but I've given it to him." She swept her hands once more across my brow, and I felt a sharp pain in my head, then a sensation like falling into something nice and warm.

"You'll need to get used to seeing more than usual," she commented. "When you open your eyes, you'll realize that I'm not what I seemed. Open up and have a look!"

Where had the old witch with the gleaming hair gone? I recognized the raven tresses, but underneath were happy blue eyes regarding me. These looked out from a pretty face, as beautiful as a rose, with a smile revealing pearly-white teeth.

If I had not worshiped my wife, I would've been pierced by Cupid's arrow immediately. At the edge of this vision were Mannul and Alberto, curled up laughing. Valencio was on the floor, his mouth gaping. Titch was with him, licking his ear to restore him to reality (doggy reality, at least!).

"What a gift you've been given!" Mannul exclaimed. "Now you'll be able to see the person inside everyone you meet! You'll become a true judge of character, Tim, and you'll see even more in the future."

I rubbed my eyes and turned to hug the beautiful witch, but there were only us visitors there: Mannul, Alberto, Val, Titch, and me. I left the cave with the two Masters as if in a trance.

There sat Old Mother Sjaluna, stirring her pot. Simultaneously, I could make out a diaphanous figure at her side — the beautiful girl from the cavern, the girl inside Sjaluna. I rushed to hug the old lady, nearly upsetting the cauldron, but she steadied it swiftly and turned on me resentfully.

"You're in too much hurry, Sisilla's husband," she hissed. "Save your mollycoddling for your wife and go on ferreting about for the aborigines next!"

My chortling companions waved farewell to her and so did Val and I. Old Mother Sjaluna didn't take any notice of us, but stayed stirring her pot of herbs.

30. With the Aborigines

The aborigines were at some distance. We had to go in the hovercraft (I called it our Rolls Royce). I had hardly awoken from the enchanted mist of Old Mother Sjaluna's, when the craft thudded to an abrupt stop.

We were in a small valley surrounded by trees. A jumble of boulders lay around, as if strewn there by a giant hand, grass pushing up between them. A wide stream, wide enough to be a river, flowed through the valley. The aborigines were everywhere, collecting water, bathing, chatting vociferously, clad in little but a loin cloth. They called and waved to us in their friendly, happy way. A tall, lithe man, his gleaming brown skin still dripping, came striding towards us. He wore a spotlessly clean, white loin cloth of minimal size.

"Welcome!" he called, reaching out a hand. "I'm Toomi. You're all very welcome. We're cooking for you over there in the clearing." He pointed towards a small boulder, but we couldn't see much. "A little bird told us you were on your way," he continued.

There were no birds involved in the deafening concert that started up. Five naked young boys were playing didgeridoos, those long wind instruments that aborigines play. Titch buried his muzzle in my arm. The music wasn't really to his taste, but it didn't last long. Then we traipsed after Toomi, who was at least seven feet tall in his bare feet, around the rocks where an amazing sight met our eyes.

A group of lovely, dark-haired girls, clad in flowers, danced and sang around a long table on which all kinds of tempting food was arrayed. I gripped Titch's collar as his eyes lit up, and wished I could've restrained Val in the same way, as he seemed inclined to throw himself on the food straight away. Luckily, he was too well brought up, in spite of his hunger, and he came and stood behind me instead.

"This is to honor our guests!" cried Toomi. "We'll say grace first, and then please eat up!"

The food-nymphs hummed gently as he called loudly and clearly, "Thank you, Eternal Father, for your grace in giving us food for ourselves and our honored guests. May all food and drink run through our bodies, rendering them fit for your divine purpose. No life has been sacrificed for this blessed feast, but Nature has supplied it from her riches! Thanks, oh thanks!"

We started in on the food, which could've been made by gods! As we were eating, I noticed something strange. Each person I looked at seemed to radiate their own aura. They were perfectly clear, in various colors. At this juncture, I didn't realize that this was an inner glow revealed to me so that I could read people like a book. This was the gift from Old Mother Sjaluna!

There was a terrified shriek from Valencio, son of the Pope. He was brandishing a lid, which he had presumably removed from one of the dishes, and was staring in horror at the serving platter. A ten-year old child, who had noticed our dismay, giggled wildly, removed a worm from the plate, and consumed it like spaghetti. It would've been fine if it had been spaghetti. No life had been sacrificed for our feast. It was true … these worms were wriggling with life! Val rushed away, probably to be sick, and I asked Mannul, who was standing nearby, what was going on. He grinned in delight.

"The aborigines eat a certain type of worm alive. It's considered a real treat. It's the only exception to Agartha's vegetarian diet. You don't have to try it. There are plenty of other dishes."

Titch and I exchanged glances. He lay down with his muzzle in his paws. It meant no. I'd lost my appetite, so the dog and I left the table, with a nod from Mannul, who didn't seem fond of worm-consumption either. The aborigines continue to eat worms to this day.

Toomi followed us, looking concerned. "I'm sorry if you didn't appreciate our food," he said, "but stay a while. We are going to dance at the edge of the forest. We have story-dances. Many of our legends are exceptionally lovely, and we have set them to music of our own composition. We will eat sun-stone bread at the same time. It's guaranteed worm-free!"

We laughed, and accepted his invitation. He took us to an open-air theater where we sat down on a grassy slope.

"We've plenty of amphitheaters in Italy," Val commented. "It's lovely here!"

At the bottom of the slope was a natural stage, surrounded by trees, with a babbling brook flowing between glistening stones. We were given bread and drink which tasted wonderful.

The beautiful dancing girls returned, graceful and gentle. Then there were trolls and creeping figures with animal-masks. The girls were scared off before our horrified eyes, and a gruesome scene replaced them. It was a war between the forces of good and evil, fought violently. It was horribly realistic, and I noticed that Val had shut his eyes.

The special effects were amazing, and body-parts — heads, arms, and legs — floated around. On closer inspection, it was apparent that puppets were used. There was a happy ending, the blaring music calmed down, and the girls returned with their cheerful dance.

Our two Masters thanked Toomi for the refreshments and entertainment and explained that we had to go. Soon we were back in the Rolls Royce, a light breeze smelling of the sea below us.

"What did we learn from the aborigines?" Val asked. "Eating worms — yuck! But it was fun, too."

"You learned how people live at one with Nature, how they create music and drama, and how they are satisfied with their lives," Mannul pointed out. "We're going home now, and we'll carry on tomorrow."

31. The Birthplace of Mankind, Africa

"Occasionally, we find ourselves in a land directly beneath the Earthly kingdom which is its birthplace," remarked Mannul, slightly obscurely, as we were sitting in the hovercraft the next day.

"Where would that be?" I wondered.

"Africa!" was the answer.

"Africa is enormous, with many lands and innumerable tribes," Valencio observed thoughtfully. "Where exactly are we going?"

"You'll see in a moment," Alberto replied in a tone of voice that brooked no argument. The craft swooped gently down onto sand sculpted by the wind into wide circles in all directions. This was unmistakably the desert.

That's all we need, I thought, a tribe from the African desert. I sat on the steps of our vehicle trying to remove the sand from Titch's muzzle. Val and the two Masters walked around this seemingly uninhabited spot, until we all heard a loud, shrill call that became more resonant.

As if from nowhere, there appeared dark-skinned warriors armed with crescent-shaped spears. They were naked, apart from loin cloths, and their skin gleamed in the sun. They were painted with white stripes and other characters, and had feathers on their heads. Some of them had feathers fastened behind, giving the impression of birds. They rolled their eyes and seemed terrifying. Val moved closer to the Masters, who were holding out their hands towards the tribe.

To my surprise, I noticed rings of light swarming around their hands like huge insects. The tribe took a step back and fell to their knees in front of Alberto and Mannul.

The rings of light had obviously made an impression. A man at least seven feet tall got up from the group and approached us. I couldn't understand what he said, but Alberto spoke to him. It was a long conversation. In the end, the tall man beckoned us to follow him, which we did.

We were still in the desert, but it was no longer empty. Small, conical huts were silhouetted against the intense blue sky, smoke arising from them.

A young woman with ebony skin and tightly-curled hair piled high on her head approached us. She was strangely beautiful in her foreign way. She wore a gold cloth at her waist, was painted in yellow and gold, and was weighed down with jewelry. She stood before the Masters, and they all bowed to each other. Gold glittered from her arms, neck, and waist, and on her feet were gold sandals laced high up her legs with gold ribbon. Her skin was even darker than the tall man's.

"This is Yola, the Gold Queen," the tall man introduced her. "You are in Uuria, the birthplace of mankind. From here all races on the Earth originated."

We could understand him, and we understood what the Gold Queen said when she started talking. We sat on the sand, and she perched on a sort of woven gold throne that was brought for her and which gleamed like the sun.

"You strangers desire to see the birthplace," she said, in more strident tones than we had expected. "This village was created so long ago that the surface of the Earth was still not formed. Heaven created us in his image. Heaven took the trouble of giving us human inheritance. We went to the surface, where we were betrayed and disappointed.

"The survivors returned here. People who we were going to confirm as true children of Heaven betrayed us with the help of the evil king's war, power, and selfishness, and he remained in power. His name was Anu and his followers were called the Annunaki. He and his followers have finally fled to their own planet.

"People on the surface will be given the chance to become what was originally intended. The children of Heaven will regain their Origin. Anu held them fettered by evil, and the evil brought darkness of thought and feeling.

"Some of the children of Heaven luckily managed to retain their generosity, Love, and integrity, and they will help us now. We have grieved for the Earth as a cherished relative, but our grief has changed to joy. We have great help from other planets and we're planning a UFO visit to enlighten the surface-dwellers about their wonderful inheritance."

"As above, so below," I interrupted her. "Where does that come from?"

"It's the very first decree which Heaven taught us," the Queen replied. "That's how it was meant to be, and will be in the future. Knowledge meant ego triumphed over spirit; that is what happened."

It was warm, like a hot summer's day on the surface. We were treated to cooling drinks and lively conversation with the attractive Queen Mother, as she turned out to be, and her court. On the surface, we don't believe that the Earth is so ancient and its culture so extensive.

Yola had a choir which sang madrigal-like songs. They were herding songs from the goat-herders. The goats had longer horns and shorter coats than we are used to, because of the heat.

The village was sizeable and scattered across a wide area. The sand dunes and the desert finished pretty much where we had landed. Long grass and flowers replaced it further on, including a cactus resembling an orchid which I had never seen before. The people were such a mixture, both black and white. Yola explained that it was Heaven's original plan that all people should live together, but that differences increased as the surface was populated.

As we entered the "town," the houses changed. Here there were more normal houses, almost like English cottages, with clay walls and thatched roofs. Chimneys didn't exist, as it was so hot, and food was cooked outside. The "kitchens" were like booths, but to judge from the food, they were perfect for cooking in.

By the time we were ready to go, we were almost overwhelmed by music, great vegetarian food, and the joy emanating from this magical place.

"Are we going to China, too?" the inquisitive Val asked.

Mannul chuckled. "Not until tomorrow. Now it's time to get home before Sisilla thinks we've gotten lost in the jungle!"

At home was another surprise. I was welcomed by my friend Chaos from Dalarna in Sweden. Behind him was my dear wife.

"I'm organizing a party," she announced. "Travelers need refreshments and food. You two can have a chat while I'm getting it ready. I've sent a message to Emilie that we have a visitor."

Chaos had quite a tale to tell. He'd already befriended Sisilla and was delighted by my life companion. I asked him how he found his way to us, and he replied, "For a while, everything was normal at home. But after you and your grandmother left, it wasn't fun anymore. Emilie and I had discussed Agartha, and I got hold of all the information I could on it. There wasn't much. Then I booked a flight to Mount Shasta, and here I am! It was a bit hairy before I reached Telos and started asking people for you. Everyone knew who you were.

"It's great here! I don't know how long I'll be staying, maybe for good! What do you think?"

"I'm sorry for your Swedish friends who will miss you, and I'm ecstatic that you've come!" I exclaimed, hugging him. I told him about the amazing, magical kingdom he had come to, and invited him to stay as long as he liked. It took half the night to recount our adventures here. Sweden seemed very far away, but Grandmother was overjoyed to see our friend and she also had much to relate.

32. A Completely Different China

Both Grandmother and I found that our memories had been renewed. This book is a product of that renewal! It's easy to forget your old life when your new one is in paradise.

The following morning, Mannul and Arniel picked us up for our next voyage into Agartha the enchanted. As far as I could understand, land and sea on the surface were paralleled by land and sea here inside. We therefore expected China to be approximately where it was on the surface.

However, nothing in Agartha is that obvious. Everything is very different than how it is on the surface. I had never actually been to China, only read about it and seen it in films.

Both Masters quickly introduced themselves to Chaos.

Grandmother and Lex came too, so my Rolls Royce was joined by another hovercraft that I referred to as the Audi. This amused Mannul and Arniel.

I don't know what I'd expected, but Titch and I alighted in the market square of a town. It was a large square, with other hovercraft parked around an attractive fountain. The Audi drew up next to the Rolls, and Chaos wobbled out, holding his head.

Flying in a hovercraft is disorientating. Laughing, I put my arm around his shoulder and Titch added his support, nudging and shoving him. My enormous dog stood on his hind legs as though surveying the situation. He had taken instantly to Chaos and probably remembered him from Sweden.

The jumbled images I remembered seeing of contemporary China were nothing like what I saw here. At one side of the lovely fountain with its two life-size dolphins, a wide, gleaming street opened up. On the other side were bright, glittering roofless houses, climbing plants, and palm trees. A river ran down the middle of the broad street. In the distance were bridges — high, hump-backed bridges, also glittering.

The people around were tall, attractive, and well-built. They were indeed dark-haired and dark-eyed, with high cheek bones, but they seemed to be made from mother-of-pearl. They were clad in fairly long cloaks in pale colors.

There was no crowding. They all walked separately, bowing continuously and smiling in all directions. If this is where China came from, I thought, the country should return to its roots.

The Masters saw our surprise. All of us had our mouths hanging open — Val, Chaos, Grandmother, Lex, and I! We couldn't have been more flabbergasted. The Masters beckoned us to hover across the street with them. The Chinese greeted us, bowing, and we tried to return their greetings as best we could. Titch gravitated to my side, raising a laugh when he bowed his head from time to time. Many Chinese had pets with them, and yet the street was quiet and peaceful. The pets were like ours, mostly cats and dogs and a few donkeys with bejeweled saddle-cloths.

We stopped by a building which resembled one of the temples painted onto old Chinese porcelain. It glowed in pinkish hues and was bathed in light. "If this is where the Chinese come from, it's changed drastically on the surface," I muttered, and the others nodded in agreement.

"The outer world has the ability to transform," Arniel assented. "That is why it must change again, in a positive way."

We entered the temple. A pleasant incense aroma greeted us. It wasn't at all like a church inside — there was no altar and no pews. Instead, there were comfortable stools on a beautiful carpet. In the center was a golden rostrum studded with precious stones. Gentle music caressed us. It was empty but for the lovely, long-haired cats lying across the stools, regarding us with feline shrewdness. They weren't upset by Titch. I held on to him just in case, but he glanced at them nonchalantly and yawned.

"You are welcome to meditate a while or just sit in quiet contemplation," Mannul explained. "We have these places all over Agartha. We call it sanctuary."

"This is exactly what we need on the surface!" Grandmother broke the silence.

"It's exactly what we're planning," Arniel commented.

"It'll take time, but great changes are coming to the Earth. Different religions must come to an end. The most sacred place is inside us and can be discovered in a space like this."

"You can sense God here," my little grandmother remarked, putting her hands together. "Amen!"

"Do you envisage God as a kind of Master?" Val asked. "I do too, actually."

"He's in another dimension watching over us constantly," Grandmother announced with conviction.

Mannul looked at her and smiled. "That's not really the image of God we have here," he pointed out gently. "God is inside us all. We only have to listen to the voice of Love. That's what Arniel meant."

Val sank down onto a stool, his head in his hands. I think he was crying. Compared to his tough religious upbringing, this was heaven-sent. Grandmother and her husband sat down too, clasping their hands as we surface-dwellers are wont to do. In the end, all of us rested on the soft, carpeted temple floor. Titch had his head in his paws and I knew he was content. Then we left.

The whole town was a great, bright joyous experience. We didn't meet any wise men or women, just happy, fulfilled people; children and adults. There weren't many traces of contemporary China to be detected in the original.

"It's the same with Japan," Arniel said. "We just wanted to show you how far negative influences have succeeded on the surface. However, each country has a soul where part of the original is preserved. That's why it's not too late to save the Earth."

"What exactly is going to happen?" Val was obstinate. He was looking for the truth.

Arniel smiled. "Preparations are taking place now; hence the hurry to show you the original. The Earth is entering a new phase, which will be full of disaster. Afterwards, the Earth won't look the same. It will be transformed and regain the enchanting beauty it once had."

"What about the people?" Val was still on the case. "What will happen to the Pope and the rest of the Vatican?"

"Their destinies depend on their own choices, my boy. Many will end up here in Agartha. Some will relocate to other planets. There will unfortunately be many deaths, but even the souls of those people have a destiny."

"I don't really want to bring my dad here," mumbled Val, "but it was a shame my Uncle Reimfort didn't like it here."

We had returned to our vehicles by this time and taken our seats, so the discussion ended.

It was a hot day, unusually so for the climate here. I pointed this out and Mannul replied.

"It's a result of climate change on the surface. We feel the difference more often now. It never used to happen. For the first time in thousands of years we are feeling the influence of all the hate and anger which pulsates on the surface and penetrates through the Earth's crust. We are still protected from the negativity radiated by the surface, but as more surface-dwellers find their way here, we are bound to feel the influence. We are forced to batten down the hatches and wait for D-day, when we will make ourselves known to the surface and try to save its inhabitants."

"I was just in time, thank goodness!" Chaos exclaimed.

"I'm hungry," Val announced, looking around the house. We had all come home in order to sit and discuss the events of the day. Only the Masters had gone.

"I'll get something to eat," said Sisilla. "Sit down at the table and there will be food."

"Can't I get the food?" Val asked, searching around the kitchen. "There's nothing to cook here! I love cooking and I've cooked a couple of times at Edmund's house, only I'm not allowed to cook meat there."

"Not here, either!" replied Sisilla hastily. "I'll create whatever vegetables you need, just tell me."

My wife and Val spent some time in secret and produced excellent food for us. Val had insisted upon boiling, frying, and roasting, with brilliant results.

"The surface has lost a great chef," I commented, patting the young man on the shoulder.

"How do you think I survived before I got here? The money I stole from the Vatican didn't last long. I cooked in a few places, learning as I went along. I know that the residents of Telos create food by thought, but I love to use my hands as well."

We enjoyed the meal, but my wife was exhausted by creating all the ingredients, some previously unknown to her.

Grandmother was most impressed, and she kept eating and kept praising Val, suggesting he should become a Master Chef.

"It was fun!" Val's entire face glowed with pride. "I'll gladly do it again. It's boring not cooking. It's so organized here. We can't just eat when we want."

Sisilla stared at him doubtfully. "We've always found that easiest," she said. "If you have a different suggestion, you should talk to the Masters. I don't think they'd stop you from doing something you enjoy. You might teach us all something!"

"Let's open a restaurant!" exclaimed Grandmother in delight. "Val can be chef. I know it would be a huge success here, even without money involved."

And that is exactly what we did, although possibly not quite as Emilie had imagined. But that is another story.

33. Another Encounter with Saint Germain

I had always found working nine to five very boring and could understand the lure of the sea for my father. It was unpredictable, exciting, and full of challenges. I'm not cut out for sitting at a desk doing accounts or organizing jobs for others which are a waste of time. I want to surge forward, altering the plan of action, helping out, and playing with wind and water. I want to be myself without it becoming an ego trip.

My new job gave me this opportunity. It also brought me the opportunity to grow, to see things in a different light, and to learn to live by cosmic laws instead of prejudiced and restrictive laws stipulated by people. I've always been interested in Life, and now I had someone to be interested with.

Mannul had prepared me for visiting Saint Germain again. Apparently I had more to learn from this wise man. While I waited for Mannul, and my wife was getting ready to come, my life up to the present ran through my mind for some reason.

When I joined my father at sea on that fateful journey, my plans for the future were all decided. I was definitely going to follow in his footsteps. I wanted to be captain of a ship, at peril of the high seas. My plans were amorphous and naive, and I knew my mother didn't want another sailor in the family. I thought I'd be able to convince her and my sister, but that's not what happened. When Mannul saved my life, my plans changed. There were new expectations, new discoveries, new targets and challenges.

My thoughts and feelings focused on fitting into a totally new life inside the Earth. Right from the beginning I loved it and didn't bother with profound spiritual problems. I'd always believed God was a positive power, without needing a religion. It worked for me. Since meeting Sisilla, Love has come to the fore. Agartha doesn't have religions, at least nothing which is forced on others. In the small temples I always feel happy and positive about life.

I've left a lot of relationships behind. I don't often think about my friends on the surface, because my beloved grandmother is here and she represents all the friends and relatives I need. I missed Chaos, but it's great now he's here.

I thought about my new friends down here.

Mannul was the first one I met, and from the moment he rescued me and I came around in the boat, we'd become firm friends and will always remain so.

Arniel is also a good friend. He has such a good sense of humor and is easy-going.

Lex and Edmund, with their Indian roots, are lovely friends who I would like to know more.

Valencio is a brilliant venture. He is like a son and is very versatile.

I considered how the short time I've been in Agartha, which is actually many years, has brought me such a lot, and I'm deeply grateful to Life for dealing me this hand and giving me the most wonderful wife in the world.

"Are you sitting and cogitating all on your own?" Sisilla laughed, hugging me. I glanced at her. She was a sight for sore eyes, hazy in shimmering white. Fresh roses replaced jewelry across her chest.

Seeing my face, she laughed again, "Don't worry about the poor flowers! I've borrowed them from a bush and I'll put them back when we return. You don't mind a bit of magic?"

It was a great honor to be meeting Saint Germain. I realized there must be good reason for him to see us; I just couldn't fathom it. I soon found out.

Saint Germain the Master was impressive. We were conducted to one of the small, bejeweled temples to be found everywhere on this strange continent. Clad in a white cloak with numerous emblems and decorations, he greeted us and invited us to be seated on a round, emerald green couch in the middle of the temple. Titch had stayed with Grandmother, just in case. His expressions of joy could be violent and undignified in such company.

"What a shame Titch isn't here," the dignified Master commented, laughing warmly.

"You may have been expecting a telling-off, but you shouldn't. You've earned the opposite, which Sisilla is beautiful living proof of. I congratulate you on your conquest of one of the loveliest girls here. Her beauty is not skin-deep, it's five-dimensional. You aren't five-dimensional yet, and that's why you're here. It is tiresome that Sisilla has to constantly transform between dimensions, but this should not separate you."

"I thought I would become five-dimensional with time," I remarked doubtfully.

"It doesn't work like that," Saint Germain said, smiling. "Being five-dimensional physically and intellectually has to be learned. This is necessary in your case. Your in-laws knew this when they approved your Love Union. Today you must make a choice. Do you want to transform to the fifth dimension and remain in Shamballa with your wife and future children, or do you want to stay in Telos where your friends are and meet your wife occasionally?"

This came as a shock, but I didn't hesitate.

"I want to transform, and live with Sisilla in Shamballa," I replied. My wife found my hand and squeezed it. Saint Germain and Mannul both beamed.

"It means being apart for a while," Saint Germain continued. "The education and treatment which Timothy needs doesn't take place here. He has to go to the House of Transformation in the mountains. He has to go at once!"

"I'd like to tell Grandmother," I remonstrated. "I can't leave without explaining why or telling her how God really is."

"Mannul will explain to her where you are and tell her that the

God within us is the only true God," the Master decided. "I'm sure she'll look after Titch for you. Valencio will help her. Sisilla will be at her parents' house while you are away. When you return, she will have found a home in the capital for you and the child."

I almost jumped out of my skin.

"What child?" I cried, staring at my lithe wife.

Sisilla crept onto my lap. "Sorry. Saint Germain got there before me!" she whispered. "I haven't told a soul, least of all him, but he knows everything!"

"You will be back in time for your son's birth!" Saint Germain smiled and I felt quite peeved. He really did know everything! "Timothy, say goodbye to Sisilla and Mannul, and then come with me."

"What about that job you offered me?" I exclaimed resentfully. "I would really like it."

"That was before you decided to become five-dimensional," Mannul consoled me. "You'll get a better job after this, and you'll be able to see twice as far. Your friends will have to decide which dimension they wish to live in, but it will take longer for them to become five-dimensional. The usual course takes place in our wonderful library, Porthologos. You will soon be reunited, but you must leave your wife just now."

It was really tough, but it couldn't be helped. I hugged her firmly. Sisilla dried a stubborn tear which had rolled down her cheek and then she left the temple abruptly. Even Mannul had gone, and I was left with the honored Master, Saint Germain. He took my hand, smiled warmly, and said, "Let's go!"

In a swift moment of swirling mist I found myself at the House of Transformation, high up in a snowy world where rays of sunshine found it difficult to penetrate the dense pine forest, only to be compared with Sweden's most northerly, most fair, and most luxuriant forest. Saint Germain and I stood side by side before a building that seemed carved out of the cliff-face itself — the grayest, most closely-veined and glinting marble I have ever come across.

34. The House of Transformation

This book should end here, but I know that the House of Transformation is a name that will whet the appetite of my readers, so I feel that you must come with me.

Everything had happened so quickly that I had no time to wonder what was waiting for me. It had all been so unexpected, so unpredictable. I followed Saint Germain in bewilderment and looked around me. The door was opened by a smiling man in a white cloak. He didn't have the shaved head of a monk. His hair cascaded in black waves to his shoulders. He bowed low to the Master and indicated with his hand the direction we should take.

We were in a light, pillared hall where the walls, doors, and roof seemed to be made of crystal. A crystal cavern, I thought. In the center of this enormous hall a fountain was playing, shooting forth multicolored water from a huge colorful shell. On closer investigation, this shell was open, glinting, rosy mother-of-pearl, with a shimmering pearl inside. It was the loveliest fountain I have ever seen.

Saint Germain smiled while I admired the fountain, and then gestured for us to continue. Breathless with delight, I enjoyed the colors from outside reflected in all the glass. We went up stairs of glass covered in shimmering green carpet to keep us from slipping. I hadn't noticed before, but there were rugs on the floor to walk on. These were soft and shimmering, and served a purpose in this glass palace.

We entered a door at the top of the stairs. This was a much smaller glass room, carefully lit. There were cushioned benches and a smooth wall of white marble, which I realized served as a screen.

In front of this was a glass rostrum like a pulpit. I recognized the couple on it. I had met them at a party in Telos. We embraced as old friends and Saint Germain observed, "This is the classroom in the House of Transformation. I'm going to leave you, Timothy, in the capable hands of your friends, and we'll meet again when you've finished." He kissed me on both cheeks. Then he left in the usual way — he just vanished.

Thus my conversion to the fifth dimension began. It was an enjoyable, exciting time, if demanding, and I never had time to be bored, even when I missed Sisilla. We would soon be together again, and I was going to be at my son's birth, as promised.

Unfortunately, I'm not allowed to tell you how I became five-dimensional, after an edifying slog. It's still classified information, but hopefully one day the whole of humanity will be able to share in this wonderful, cleansing experience.

Joy is a major part of it — nothing boring. Continuous joy, laughter, song, music, dance, and the easy unity of the body and soul make life indescribably happy.

My dear reader, if you don't believe what I have told you in this book, sit silently and listen to your Inner Voice. You will hear this in your own head and feel it in your heart if you seriously want to know if Agartha really exists. I assure you it does, but why believe me? You can find out for yourself. The time is coming when Agarthans will come to the surface as living proof.

I'm laughing now! Gravity and humor co-exist. Sometimes seriousness spills over into laughter, but hardly ever the reverse. Lighten up about your dignity, your capacity for influencing others, which is a form of control, and your wish to remain non-committal about belief and knowledge.

Recognizing the God within you should go without saying. God = the person or force in what you call heaven, an endless mass of constellations and planets of uninhabited gas bubbles. I'm telling you, God is everywhere. God is in your wonderful surroundings which we want to conserve for the future, in the flora and fauna outside your house which are so natural you no longer notice them.

The whole of this beautiful, divine Creation is being totally destroyed by people. This is a distressing image of the planet's surface. Should we accept it? We can't. The cosmos is reacting. A Cosmic Council exists, unknown to us. It won't accept that this blindingly lovely planet Earth is rent asunder by filthy hands seeking power and riches, instead of taking care of what there is.

Dear reader, this book is to awaken a new consciousness in you, so that in these troubled times you can LOVE the world. Think how you can help, and leave behind your apathy and selfishness. Love and empathy are the first steps on the road we must take. There are six other steps besides: Appreciation, Compassion, Forgiveness, Humility, Understanding, and Valor. Practice these six heart virtues and you will feel the fine winds of change embrace your body and soul!

I, Timothy, from the fifth dimension and Agartha, the eighth continent, have told you my story truthfully and passionately. Every word I have uttered is true, and through my medium, Mariana, I have brought the whole of humanity greetings from another kingdom: Agartha greets all brothers and sisters and looks forward to a future of joyful, friendly co-operation.

35. Author's Epilogue

I realize that many readers will doubt that Agartha really exists. So far it is very difficult to prove, but remember that in the past we stubbornly believed the world was flat …

Timothy has been my friend. He first appeared in my home when I was sitting on my meditation sofa. I could see him clearly for a fraction of a second, and I'm not one to hallucinate. He was a young man, of Nordic appearance, tall and blond, with a lovely, friendly face and strange, penetrating blue eyes. I didn't have time to see much more, but perceived that he was wearing white trousers and a white, ribbed polo-neck. I could hear him quite clearly in my head:

"My name's Timothy. Originally I'm from Seattle, but I live in Agartha these days," he said, "the world inside the Earth. The Earth is hollow, don't you know? Agartha is a huge kingdom with many entrances, one of which is on Mount Shasta in California. The reason people don't know about this world is that we've kept it secret to protect it. We don't want war or environmental toxins here like on the surface. We've created a toxin-free, moneyless, flowering landscape, and we want to keep it that way.

"The day is coming when we will contact you people on the surface, and you must write this book as preparation. Some people have already discovered us, including Admiral Richard E. Byrd.

"If you read this book, you will have some insight into the Truth and Love which are our realities. You will see how we live and it will be easier to understand. There are other books about Agartha in English, by Dianne Robbins: *Telos* and *Messages from the Hollow Earth.*"

15 Author: Epilogue

Books by Mariana Stjerna

Mariana Stjerna is a highly respected Swedish channel and author. She has been psychic since childhood and has written several spiritual books both for adults and children. *On Angels' Wings* is the English publication of her Swedish breakthrough novel *På Änglavingar*. Other examples of her international releases include *Time Journey to the Origin and the Future, The Bible Bluff, The Invisible People, Agartha – The Earth's Inner World,* and *Mission Space.*

In her novels Mariana Stjerna gives important paradigm-breaking information and knowledge presented in an easily accessible and entertaining way. Enjoy!

For more info on Mariana Stjerna's books, visit www.SoulLink.se. Paperback and ebook (Kindle) versions are available on Amazon.

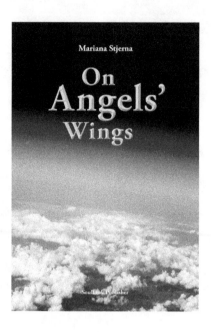

Are you afraid of dying? Do you believe that life ends with your last breath? This book is the story about what happened to the famous Swedish author Jan Fridegård after his passing. Through his spokesperson, Mariana Stjerna, he tells vividly with both humor and seriousness his experiences on "the other side."

The reader is invited to join Jan on an amazing journey *On Angels' Wings* to different worlds and realms throughout our widespread cosmos. Some highlights: Crossing Over, The Akashic Records, Creation, The Nine Elders of Sirius, No Man's World, Astral Realms, Midnight Mass, The Angelic Realm, Shamballa, Ashtar Command, Helia and Sananda. The book also contains a Cosmic Map of the different kingdoms, with the Great Spirit in the middle.

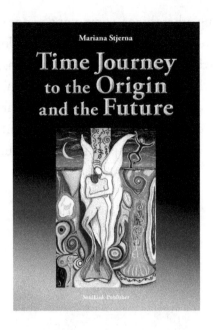

Time Journey to the Origin and the Future is the independent sequel to Mariana Stjerna's well received novel *On Angels' Wings*. While the former book is about what happens to us after our physical death, this book discloses the origin of man and what will happen to Earth and humanity when we have passed through the Grand Portal, become wiser, and achieved a higher consciousness.

In his own special way Jan Fridegård continues, through his writing medium Mariana Stjerna, to tell about his missions and adventures on the other side. This time he gets to make a time journey far beyond our own universe.

"It's time for you to not only visit unknown planets or parts of our infinite beingness. You will travel into what one might call the future. … It will be a mystical journey across all boundaries – I mean technically feasible boundaries, seen from a human perspective. Now you have to throw off all your prejudices and put on a shimmering garment, which brings you into something that you in your wildest dreams could never have imagined," said Master Melchizedek when he informed us about the mission. "This journey is a lesson about what the cosmos really is, – or the original cosmology, if you think that sounds better."

We may, among other things, come along to one of the seven Super Universes, which revolve around a static Central Universe, and make visits to the following cultures of origin: the Mayas, the Maoris, the Incas, the Aztecs, the Sumerians, the Inuits, the Zulus, the Etruscans, the Basques, etc., all of which have been or still are represented on Earth. The book concludes with a visit to the Central Race and the WingMakers, who are living in a paradise … without violence, female maltreatment, lust for power, or greed.

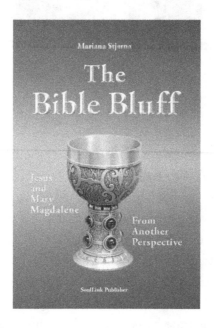

The Da Vinci Code tells us that Jesus and Mary Magdalene were a couple and had children together. Is that really correct? Did Jesus die on the cross or did he not? What about the Immaculate Conception? Why was Reincarnation removed at the meeting in Constantinople in the year 553? What function did the Grail have, and is it true that Joseph of Arimathea collected the blood of the crucified Jesus in it? Where is the Grail now, and what mission will it have for humanity in the future? Who was the real Mary Magdalene – a whore or a saint? Was she perhaps the mother of the women's liberation movement?

You will find the answers to these questions and much more in this book. Here is a new version of the life of Jesus and what happened in biblical times. The author's spiritual contact has visited these times and has amazing things to tell. It is time for the Truth to be revealed the way it has been told to those who listen. But it is up to the reader to listen to their inner Truth, which is hidden in their heart.

Do you know that invisible beings, Nature spirits, of the most various kinds exist in Nature, and that every one of them has a special task?

Unfortunately, most of us don't know this, and moreover, we only *believe* in things which we can see with our physical eyes. Fortunately, there are those who are able to see behind the veils we generally have in front of our eyes …

Through our ignorance we kill and scare off these elementals with our toxins, our violence, and our insensitivity, which already have had dire consequences. But it has not always been so. Once, a long time ago, humans cooperated with the elementals in harmony and balance, and to this unity we must return.

In this book, the writer's spiritual inspirer, Jan, together with a religious historian and two elves, will make peep-holes into different ages – from about 20 million years ago and forward – in the greatest, most magical, and secretive of all worlds: Nature. The mission is to inform humans about the magic of Nature and also to investigate when, where, and how humans, elves, and Nature spirits cooperated in good spirit. The time journeys are always started from Mother Earth's beautiful green cave in the innermost of the Earth.

At the end of the book are included a number of channeled messages from Pan, the uncrowned ruler and King of Nature.

Mariana Stjerna has, ever since her childhood, had a deep feeling for Nature and the elementals, both of which she has experienced and communicated with and still does. The time is now ripe to tell about this magical but so far invisible world, which exists right next to us. This is the fourth book inspired by Jan Fridegård.

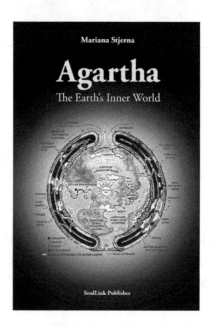

In Medieval times, people believed the Earth was flat and that the sun rotated around it. The Catholic Church considered it heresy to suggest that the Earth was round and orbited the sun. The astronomer Copernicus was aware of this, and did not dare publish his findings until on his death-bed in 1543.

The next major "disclosure" is revealed in this book. The Earth is hollow and populated by an advanced race, who is planning to come to the aid of people on the surface very soon. Will this concept be accepted by scientists and the religious community? Is this science-fiction, fantasy, or liberation? We can only advise you to read this book, written as a novel, and examine your own heart.

There are those who have already visited Agartha, the world inside the planet, and found society there advanced and flourishing. Admiral Richard E. Byrd, USA (1947) is one of them. He was not given to flights of fancy.

Mariana Stjerna made contact with Timothy Brooke, a Canadian, who appeared to her briefly and then "dictated" this book. He was saved by Agarthans from a shipwreck off the coast of Canada in the mid-20th century, and is now alive and well in Agartha. In this book, he recounts his story and describes life in this five-dimensional paradise.

Mariana's well-received book, *Agartha – The Earth's Inner World,* had just been released (2010) when she had a visitation from her cosmic friend and source of inspiration, Jan Fridegård, who told her he, too, had been to Agartha. He gave an account of his experiences there in the company of his dear friend and companion Lydia, whom we've met in a couple of previous books. They had also been on exciting adventures out in Space to the Pleiades, Sirius B, and Andromeda. Did Mariana wish to be his writing medium again? Of course!

In Agartha, they visit Porthologos, which houses a most extraordinary, gigantic library (with no books) that is several miles in length, wherein all human knowledge is contained. All one has to do is choose what one wishes to learn about, and in an instant, seemingly live holographic images appear, presenting the subject in question in a lifelike manner.

In Agartha they meet the enigmatic Pilgrim, who imparts much of his immense wisdom to them and acts as their guide on several of their journeys. Among many other wonderfully fascinating places, they visit an intriguing research center, the Fortress, where notable inventions and discoveries evolve, and to which many eminent researchers from the surface world have been transferred, such as Darwin and Tesla.

On the Pleiades (the Seven Sisters, comprised of many advanced Galactic Societies) no large cities exist, only very small communities in which virtually everyone knows one another and enjoys being in each other's company. Interesting accounts are given regarding the Pleiadean Parliament, their school system, and general way of living. Janne and Lydia also learn about its wildlife and sea people. Truly – this isn't a misprint – mermaids really do exist. ... On Sirius B they make the acquaintance of a dolphin community, besides the amphibians – who have fish-suits. They further are privileged to experience a wondrously stupendous Evening song in the Ivory Cave.

The journey ends in Andromeda, where all individuals are part of a higher consciousness, and life seems easy to live. They are shown healing houses, and even manage to visit a reptilian planet before returning to Agartha and its capital, Shamballa.

For more info on Mariana Stjerna's books, visit www.SoulLink.se. Paperback and ebook (Kindle) versions are available on Amazon.